Forever And Always

Kate Sparrows

Kate Sparrows; kate.sparrows@gmail.com
https://www.facebook.com/kjsparrows

Publisher's Note: This is a work of fiction. Names, characters, places, and incidents are a product of the author's imagination. Locales and public names are sometimes used for atmospheric purposes. Any resemblance to actual people, living or dead, or to businesses, companies, events, institutions, or locales is completely coincidental.

Cover Design: Melody Pond; http://melodyypond.weebly.com
Printed by CreateSpace, An Amazon.com Company

Forever And Always/ Kate Sparrows. -- 1st ed.
ISBN 978-1-943797-03-5

Being deeply loved by someone gives you strength, while loving someone deeply gives you courage.

— LAO TZU

Chapter One

Ava's death was just another suicide on the fourth page of the newspaper. It fit in inconspicuously amongst the other deaths which included old age and one other suicide, in the form of an overdose. It made her out to be just another overworked young woman who gave into the everyday troubles that ultimately resulted in taking her own life. But for the dark haired man that stood a few feet behind her family, watching the casket being lowered into the ground and out of his sight, he knew suicide was the last thing she'd do. And maybe because of that, the news had come as such a shock and the matter of her remains dealt with so quickly. The sting of her sudden departure screamed to be hidden beneath the earth.

Jack Havest had known the auburn haired firecracker for just over three years. He had been working on figuring out a better way to increase the lifespan of rail when she stopped by his cubicle. But for some reason as she stood there next to his superior as they were introduced, there was a feeling that they just had to know each other and the others hurrying around the office disappeared for a moment.

It hadn't taken long to befriend Ava Koltrin. At first, the meetings near her cubicle down the hall were slightly awkward. She had to think he was just another creeper the way he'd peek his head over the cubicle wall. He had tried to be sneaky about it and he'd walk in after seeing she was there. But that seemed to have changed quickly before the week was over. She was easy to talk to, even if she was more reserved in her choice of words. But there was something about her that made Jack want to tell her everything. And that was something that hadn't dissipated over the years.

Their harmless chit-chat had turned into lunches and into working as close to each other as possible. Looking back now, it was funny to think that a few of the older men in the department had pegged them as a couple long before they had even thought about it themselves. Ava had admitted later that one particular old man had started to tease her a few days after she started work. Of course she thought he was just a crazy old gossip who was trying to get her goat.

For Jack it had been nothing but suspicious looks when they were seen talking to each other, even if it was for a moment or simply saying good morning as they passed each other in the hall. He had just decided that they were still not used to seeing a new person around the office. Being a friendly co-worker was the excuse he had used a few times to calm things back down and to stop Ava from catching on. It wasn't until later that Ava had told him about the sly comments that were mentioned within earshot or hinted at that he failed to notice. He had laughed it off knowing most of them already and raising an eyebrow at some he hadn't heard.

The hand of Ava's father on his shoulder as the aging man passed with down-trotted eyes snapped Jack out of his thoughts of those earlier, happier times. The two shared a moment of painful understanding before leaving Jack alone next to the grave. They had both lost someone dear. Someone who wouldn't let herself be easily replaced, even if that was possible. There was no one near as special as she had been. Maybe if the technology ever became advanced enough to merge people together. But then it was still debatable.

Even though he was alone with Ava now, he couldn't urge his feet to take him nearer to her. The body in that wooded box wasn't the girl he knew. That person was a cold shell of a lively person. Although the funeral had been closed casket, the scene inside couldn't have been a pleasant one. There was no way anyone would want to remember her that way. And no one except those who dealt with or heard the gossip of fatalities knew what she probably looked like now.

Instead of accepting the fact that she broke her promise to never leave him, he couldn't let her go nor go to her now. It was just like those first few months. Like forbidden fruit in the Garden of Eden. The temptation drawing you close while the pain lurked in the nearby shadows. Ava would always cling to his thoughts as long as he lingered in this town or cling to the things they enjoyed, like their hot cocoa movie nights.

But the pain of returning to work tomorrow and feeling her absence again was more tolerable than staring at the hole in the ground. As Jack turned to head towards his car parked on the side of the road, the forgotten cell phone in his dark suit's pocket rang out. He pulled out the phone only to see who was calling. Again the name read that of his parents. They had called every day since Jack broke the news to them and spent the holiday alone instead of keeping their plans at his parent's home. That was a little over a week ago. He never answered the phone since, unless it was the phone at the office. And even then it was a number known only to his co-workers. His parents probably wanted to make sure he hadn't taken his own life, but the one-liner emails he sent every day reassured them of that. Instead of talking about some amusing thing in the news or event coming up with Ava, all he had now was three words. And he recited them over and over.

I am fine.

Chapter Two

Monday morning gave no hint of what transpired the day before or even a week prior. The trains were running on schedule up and down the Atlantic Coast. The station on 30th Street was bustling with activity as normal. The Amtrak police patrolled downstairs while Jack gazed out over the activity below from the walkway that connected the two halves of the station. It was something Ava found amusing. They would watch the people below in the station. She had laughed and joked that they were ninjas or spies. The special explosive glass catching curtains had partially hidden them from the unsuspecting victims below. But now it seemed pointless to stop and Jack had tried to avoid using the crossway. Instead, he'd take the elevator down and walk across the station to take the elevator up. But today he had fallen back into his normal routine and found himself on that walkway as he walked to his office space.

That wasn't the only place Jack avoided at work. He refused to walk straight down the hall and past her cubicle. But sometimes, like this morning, it was unavoidable. It was the path he had taken for years now. Cross the walkway, head down the hall past her cubicle and to his own. Without doing so, Jack wouldn't have noticed a new name plate sticking up on the partition wall today. Jack peeked over the wall moments later to see a disgruntled face staring back at his. "What are you doing? Being some kind of creeper?"

He muttered an apology before walking around the wall and into the barren office space. A stout man with a thick graying mustache spun in the chair to face him. "I used to stop by and saying hello to the girl who used to be in this cube. I guess it's just out of habit now."

The annoyance lessened from the man's face. "You're the fifth person to stop by looking for this girl since I moved in here this morning." He spun back around to finish unpacking the things that he undoubtedly took from his last location within the building. The computer monitor was just starting up and the man quickly typed in his password when prompted. Like so many others, he used an easy to remember phrase, and just watching his eyes gave it away on a small post-it note partially hidden under the keyboard. "So what's up with this girl? Did she quit or get some fancy promotion?"

Jack shook his head. "She died. Last week." It was all he could get out without really letting his mind think about it. It was hard to keep the emotion out of it. There were too many nights being kept up by the memories and tears that seemed to flow too easily. Even though the man wasn't as disgruntled now and seem oblivious to Jack's presence, it still felt oddly familiar being in this particular cubicle again; like there was an odd presence here tugging at those loose clinging bandages that kept him together. And any minute Ava would have appeared with a cup of coffee in her hands or a stack of drawings and track charts.

"Ava Koltrin." That was all the man whose nametag read Charles Dolfry said. From Jack's spot, he could see the email the man was reading from the bright monitor. The same mass email was probably in his inbox too waiting to deliver the depressing news yet again. "No wonder she killed herself." The man mused to himself. It was hard to imagine what Charles Dolfry meant. What did he know about Ava? He didn't even know her name or what kind of person she was. And even though he had quickly judged her, Ava wouldn't have judged him and probably would have ended up befriending the man. "It looks like she was coming to work high as a kite. She probably was going to fail the drug test and couldn't take being fired."

The man wasn't too keen on having someone read over his shoulder. But the strange news had prompted him to invade the Charles' personal bubble. Jack picked up on the hints after skimming the email and backed up. That and the constant reminder she was gone and things were different now, was getting too much that Jack wandered back to his own space. Sitting down, he booted his computer and opened his email. And sure enough, the weekly newsletter was waiting. He scrolled down the page until he spotted her name.

'Ava Koltrin, Project Engineer – Special Track Engineer, passed early Tuesday morning on the platforms at Amtrak

30th Street Station in Philadelphia, PA. The station's security cameras picked up footage of her walking downstairs by way of the employee stairwell and to the platform that the 9:28am Keystone service from Harrisburg was arriving. The train engineer reported a suspicious person on the platform hiding behind the columns. As the train entered the station, Koltrin jumped down onto the track.

The Amtrak police were the first to respond and redirected passengers from the scene. Upon investigation, it was determined that Koltrin had elevated levels of alcohol, amyl nitrates and methamphetamine in her system. It is undetermined how she managed to come to be on the platform without drawing suspicion and employees are encouraged to be ever on the alert for suspicious behavior. Management and supervisors will also be randomly screened for substances starting next week.'

There was more of the article, but skimming through it seemed only to enforce the severity of drug use and the policy that was already implemented. Other than that, it seemed to put her in light of being a drug addict. Not once in the three years Jack knew her had Ava ever tried drugs nor drank more than one glass of wine or beer. And that was even a rare occasion. It was more suspicious as to the story the police were telling, but it seemed that every rule was written in blood. This just happened to be hers.

The newsletter was just sent to the trash bin. There was no point in having a reminder every time a new email popped up. Just having it at a mouse click away was too tempting. For once he was just going to have to separate his personal life from the one he had at work, which was a blurry line that Ava seemed to have walked.

Jack read through the other new messages that had come in over the weekend, but something seemed to nag at him. There really was no reason for it and there was work to be done. With deadlines approaching, there was no time to dwell on things. And it seemed as if he wasn't the only one who knew that his mind was lagging. As if on cue, the cadence that could only belong to one aged man possessing a grey beard and a wooden cane grew closer until it stopped behind him.

"So how's the research coming? I heard you were in Harrisburg at the steel factory Monday. I'm interested to know if Steelton's new cooling method really does increase the life span." And there it was. That was what the nagging feeling was about.

He had been at the meeting with the steel companies all day Monday and spent the night in Harrisburg. He had been on that train when Ava jumped. He hadn't paid much attention to the announcement when the police asked everyone to remain inside the train. It had seemed like an odd thing to announce at first, but it was only a fleeting thought. A newly created playlist had distracted his ears while things were taken care of outside as he sat in the aisle seat. And after stepping on the platform, there was no reason to glance down towards the north end they came from. He had wanted to dart upstairs to escape into his cubicle for a while. There had probably been some plan to stop by Ava's, but he couldn't remember if he ever did or what he thought when he found her missing.

And now he seemed to be analyzing her death as if it would change something. If she had jumped with a train going at that slow of speed with it entering the station there was no way it wasn't extremely painful, not that dying or being hit by a fast train wasn't painful. He wouldn't know from experience, but it wasn't hard to guess that it would be painful. Her death would have been slow judging by what he had gathered. As with every death, some sort of story got around and he could imagine what happened in her last minutes.

He could picture her standing on the platform leaning against one of the columns. It wasn't out of the ordinary for her. When they had to catch a train to a field location or conference, she had done the same thing. But would she have casually leaned against the concrete with a carefree smile on her face like the one she had as they shot the breeze? And then the train would roll in, slowing to a stop along the platform, getting ready to swap passengers on the train for those waiting patiently. She had to have watched it before jumping. Did she even think there could have been a different way to handle whatever was going on? Ava could have spoken to him about anything. And in the past, she never kept anything that really bothered her from him. It was impossible for her to lie about anything being wrong. A cute little dimple would sneak out if she tried or even thought about lying. He would have known right away if something was amiss or she was hiding something. Especially something like planning her own suicide.

Suicide was something that he never pegged her for doing. But obviously he was gravely mistaken.

And once she jumped, did she regret it and try to get out of the way? He knew that Ava heard the stories and knew what a train was possible of doing to a person. There was no doubt that the head engine would have hit her and knocked her down. Then there was really only two ways she could have been killed. Either she was hit by the machinery under the train and dragged along until death came slowly. Or the train wheels ran over her body, cutting it in half and cauterizing her flesh from the pressure as it did so. Not that the second option was any faster or less painful. And it was hard to think about her death without feeling a little like he was planning it. As if somehow, at a future date, he'd create her demise this way. Her funeral had been a closed casket and no one had mentioned what she looked like, which was best for her unknowing family and non-railroad friends.

"Well?" The short chuckle snapped Jack back to the matter at hand. With her gone, he was more distracted than when she'd steal his attention. And trying to rationalize her irrational decision was causing more bouts of zoning out than normal. "Too early in the morning or do you need another cup of coffee to function?"

"The conference was nice. You know, they want to sell us their rail with the new methods. Let us be the ones to test it and be the guinea pigs. What they discussed about extending rail life seemed to make sense, but I'm not completely sold on the idea. And it seems like a bad idea to be the first to test it when we run passenger trains running over 100 miles per hour." Jack's boss seemed to be satisfied but also had a smirk that tipped Jack off that he wasn't told everything.

"Found this when you were out." He handed over a disk in a paper sleeve. "Apparently this is how they treat their rail in Europe to withstand high speed. It might help in your research. Or in the very least give you something to do for a while." And with that the pattering of loafers dissipated down the hall.

It wasn't the first time that the old man had pulled a fast one on him. After four years, Jack still hadn't been able to completely outwit the old geezer. There always seemed to be a little bit more to the whole picture. In this case, it happened to be data from other high speed railroads using specially treated steel similar to what he had been looking at. Of course there were differences between Europe and the east coast, the types of trains used and operating speeds.

Jack slid the disc out of the sleeve and pushed the eject button on the tower of his docked laptop. The drive popped out, but there seemed to be something sticking haphazardly out of it. Something that shouldn't have been there. Where a disk would normal sit, a scrap of paper was folded up and taped to the plastic drive, probably so it wouldn't get stuck inside the computer. He peeled back the tape after setting down the disk on his desk. It was a little unnerving to think someone had tampered with his computer. But with the security measures and the high level of difficulty he choose for passwords, he doubted they would have gotten really far. And if they had, there was nothing secretive that would have been accessible to them. Or that would have been easily decrypted without knowing the style he took his notes.

He carefully unfolded the note. With just a typical cubicle, anyone could have slipped in and hid the note. But as he unfolded the paper, he could see bits of words that had bleed through the paper. It wasn't until it was completely unfolded and resting on his desk that the feeling of complete and utter sickness fell on him. It had to be some sick and twisted joke from a co-worker. But in the brief moments he humored the idea, no one would be so cruel to do this. His eyes slowly scanned the note, making their way to the beginning of the half cursive, half printed words.

Chapter Three

'I don't know how many cups of coffee I drank to stay awake last night. I hated the thought of waking up and realizing it had all been just a dream. But something pulled me into slumber and the next day was just as I feared. I knew it was going to end up being one day closer to the end for me. For us.

My world was once more filled with secrets and the fear. It was never my intention to get you caught up in this Jack, but you're the only one I know who won't settle for their lies. We both know I won't, didn't, kill myself. You're the only one I can trust. I know this might seem like a sick joke, but it's not.

I really wish I could have just embraced you one last time. I had just a glimpse of you as I arranged for these to fall into your hands and that is enough for me. I managed to see your smile one last time, even though I wasn't the one that put it there. But no matter what, I want you to be happy and forget about me. You need to move on and I'm going to make sure you keep that smile I love so much. So you can both throw this note away and not open the box at your apartment door or you can promise to stay with me until the end.'

As he read the small note, it was hard not to notice the water stains that dotted the paper. There was no doubt that she was feeling the same as he was now. The only difference was that she had probably cried freely where he was at work and unable to do so without drawing unwanted attention. Grabbing the note, he moved down the hall to the men's bathroom. Luckily no one occupied the stalls until he shut out the world behind the stark white door. It was the only place in close proximity that he could escape.

Jack read the note again. He hoped that there was some secret in the note that he missed the first time through. Or maybe that his mind was playing an evil, twisted trick on his mind. But the scrap of paper only showed the added tears that had now escaped from his face. *Why are you doing this to me Ava*, he thought. Just the existence of this note meant she planned for this all to happen. Which meant she had committed suicide after all and that she obviously didn't trust him enough after all they went through to talk to him first.

He crumbled up the note and flushed it down the toilet he had been sitting on for the past who knew how long. The betrayal had gotten to him and was poisoning the fond memories that he was left with of her. Opening the stall, he watched as one of his friends walked in. Why couldn't she do this to *him*? But then again, would he really not want to know? Not to get these last bits of her? Was that something he could live without? Of course not knowing about their existence would help. And this was only the first of some hidden amount that Ava planned for him.

"What the hell Jack? You look terrible." He watched as the shorter, blonde man stopped from going into another stall. "Are you feeling alright?" There was concern on his buddy's face. It seemed that everyone assumed he was going to either do something or fall to pieces. Not that he'd let the later show.

Was he just *alright*? "I'm fine. Probably just coming down with a cold or something." He muttered, washing his hands and dabbing some cold water on his face. What was he expected to say? That Ava's death had taken a huge toll on him after being with her for three years and now she was sending him messages from the dead, telling him she was more or less murdered? It was hard enough thinking it was a suicide. And right now that's what he wanted to believe. That was something more easily accepted than things she had in her life spiraled out of control, even though her suicide was devastating enough. But the fact that someone wished her dead and was walking free, what was he to think? By now there was no way to find who had done it even if he wanted to hunt them down.

"Alright, I'll believe you for now." He watched as his friend disappeared into the stall. He was about to leave when he heard the voice calling back out to him. "But I'll be there for you when you decide to stop lying to yourself, mate. I'm not stupid and I know what she meant to you. Just glad it wasn't after this weekend. It would have been worse for you and your parents too."

Jack pushed out of the bathroom. So much for the escape he had hoped for. It seemed to have only brought him further down. But for the damage his buddy did, he also raised a good point that Jack hadn't even thought about yet. There was no doubt when the restaurant would call to confirm his reservation Friday morning that he would remember and probably crumble. It was something that he hadn't even told his parents. The only one who knew was his best man he left in the bathroom stall and her father who would have wagered a guess after Jack had asked permission to take her hand. Ava had been more old-fashioned with concern to relationships and he had also thought it right to ask first.

Unlike her mother who was first displeased with their friendly innocent dates, her father had been more accepting and seemed to secretly be on his side. Of course, his wife came around but it seemed like she had doubts and was waiting for them to fail. Ava had jested with her stories of how both her mother, and then her friends, had plotted to marry her off. Of course it had started while Ava was still in high school, but her mother seemed more hell-bent on it after they started to hang out at work. It was almost scary to think she knew way back then that they'd end up being this serious. And for a while he pondered the thought that the woman was either psychic or just unnerving like that.

Jack slipped back into his swivel office chair. He was going to have to go out and do something to get his mind off things this weekend. Getting drunk out of his mind was an option, albeit not a good one. But sitting home alone, picturing the two of them enjoying dinner at some restaurant and him moving around the table to whisper something into her ear, was one of the things he didn't want to let his thoughts to linger on. Something that she would have thought to be related to whatever they were discussing because he was either losing his voice or wanting to keep the little tidbit a secret. He would whisper into her ear, softly brushing against her skin as he spoke, that he loved her before getting down on one knee. It was something he had tried to plan out even though he knew the romantic bar was raised if he had gone through with it. Ava would have married him if he just popped over her cubicle wall one day and asked her. She loved the hopeless romantic stuff but she loved him more and he knew that.

Chapter Four

It was almost dreadful to walk from the trolley stop towards his apartment. Even though he knew he was going to give up Ava's game and let her go. There was no point in holding on to the past or the futures that would never blossom into anything more than fantasy. And Ava had given him the easy out. She had told him yet again to be happy even if it was without her. Just like when they had started, she always thought he'd be happier with someone else.

His fingers were wrapped around the keys in his fall jacket. The trees had turned already and the weather chilled enough to warrant a scarf too. Jack stopped in the lobby to grab his mail and loosened the scarf. He stared into the mail slot for a few minutes, confused. There was supposed to be a package. Even though he wasn't going to play the game, he still was curious as to what Ava had sent. He flipped through the few pieces of mail he had in case there was a note from the building manager telling him to pick it up someplace else, but there was nothing. Maybe it was for the best there was nothing. Jack sighed as he headed up the stairs towards his place. There was the mixed emotion of being disappointed at finding nothing and the relief that maybe there was nothing more to this than her passing and a sick joke.

He turned the corner at the top of the stairs and froze as he saw a thin package leaning against his door. "What the hell?" He leaned down to pick it up as he came to his door. There was no return address on the paper bag wrapped box, just his last name and apartment number. That had to mean it was hand delivered. And Ava was dead which meant someone else knew about this game and was putting him through hell and pulling him back.

Jack stuck the key into the lock and disappeared inside. He tossed the package on the counter with the other mail on the way to the kitchen. He grabbed a beer out of the fridge and downed half of it before walked over and staring at the box. Did he dare open it? That would undoubtedly lead him down a painful path that he already decided he wanted no part of. But was he capable of just tossing the box in the trash?

He sighed, sitting down and grabbing the box. It seemed innocent enough. Shaking it didn't give away any secrets and neither did turning it over in his hands. There couldn't be too much harm in just seeing what it was before tossing it out, right? Jack slipped a finger under one of the corners and popped it up. He tore the paper off and let the contents fall into his hand.

It was a VHS tape with a strip of masking tape and scribbled words. *Election-Congressman S. Whitmore.* Jack set it down on the table puzzled over why she'd send him footage from the past election. He had voted and was sure to have seen whatever was on this tape. It was odd for Ava to have watched some 'boring politic game of whose horse is bigger'. That and she knew he didn't have a VHS player. The only one he knew about was at her place. Sure he had a key and could drive over to use it, but today was already a rollercoaster of an emotional ride.

Jack left it on the counter to actually prepare something for dinner. It wasn't too hard to pull the leftovers in a take-out container from the refrigerator and pop it into the microwave. He took swigs from the bottle as the timer ticked down. It was harder to just toss the tape out, which was probably the idea behind it. If it was some note or something like that, it probably wouldn't have been as hard. But the fact she had purposely gone out of her way to tape something that was out of her character had to mean something. Besides, what did this have to do with her committing suicide?

He had decided to stop by tomorrow after work as the microwave buzzed. Jack grabbed the extra pair of chopsticks the restaurant has sent when he had the food delivered. There had seemed to be no motivation or energy after hearing about Ava's death. Sitting in front of the TV, Jack tried to get his mind off that tape and his spoiled future as he flipped through channel after channel. To his dismay, nothing seemed to capture his interest and it was easier just to call it an early night. Although it would end up being another restless night of staring at the ceiling for him.

Chapter Five

A delicious aroma drew him out of bed. It felt like an invisible hand was leading his sleepy form down the hall towards the kitchen. "Ava?" He rubbed his eyes knowing what he was seeing was impossible. "What are you doing here?"

A soft smile grew across her face as she covered the distance between them. "I thought you might like breakfast." He felt the familiar tingle on his lips as she kissed him before turning back towards the stove. His hand gently ran over his lips. Somehow, as impossible as it was, Ava was alive and still very much real. Did that mean these clues were just a test or some twisted joke of hers? It didn't seem like a prank she'd knowingly put everyone through with the amount of pain that was felt all around.

"How can you be here?" Jack moved behind her and wrapped his arms around her, burying his face in her hair. Not that it mattered much. Not with the fact that she was here and he could hold her in his arms again. Things could go back to how they were and soon they'd be on their way to spending the rest of their lives together.

She laughed and flipped the pancake from the pan onto a plate where a small stack was forming. God, he loved that laugh and the faint smell of peppermint that laced her soft skin. There was no doubt that Ava was the one in his arms.

"I'll always be with you Jack." Her hands gently covered his own. "As long as you want me." She said softly. A slight sadness hung on her words. After all these years did she really still doubt his feelings for her? Friday night, at the latest, she would realize that he didn't want to be with anyone else.

"Ava, I'll always want to be with you. I-" Jack bolted upright in bed. Glancing around, he found his bed sheets in a tangled, discarded mess on the floor in the semi-darkness. The only sound other than his heavy breathing was the buzzing of the alarm next to his bed.

He shut off the annoying little machine that had interrupted happier moments and pulled his body from bed. Part of him knew it was just a dream, while the other still held onto the hope that she lingered somewhere. But after following the same path in the dream on his own clumsy feet, he found the kitchen empty and the aroma of peppermint mixed amongst fresh coffee and breakfast gone.

Weeks later and he was still struggling to let it go. Maybe he should talk to someone about what he was going through. There was no doubt that it wasn't the first suggestion on everyone's mind. It probably wasn't a good idea to go at it completely alone. But talking about it made him feel too vulnerable and it wouldn't bring her back or solve anything. If nothing else, it would get him over her and cause her to be erased from his life. And that wasn't something he really wanted. Maybe it was something he needed but catching a glimpse of the tape, he knew it wasn't something he could easily give up. But Ava had promised an end. And a happy one for him at that too, knowing her.

He slumped back to his bedroom. It was the same routine of waking up, getting dressed and catching the trolley to work. But now his movements were forced. What had started as a note had grown into a mysterious package and yearning dream, and became an obsession that kept him going. But it was hard to know if it was the obsession with the truth or the hope of finding another message after the VHS tape that was going to get him through the day. But nonetheless, that didn't change the fact that Ava was dead and he had five minutes to get dressed and catch the trolley.

Chapter Six

It took almost an hour to get to Ava's place using the public transportation. Not because she lived that far away, but because their scheduling was terrible. He'd just get off the bus that took him to the subway station to find it had departed no more than a minute ago. And then it was a ten minute ride on the subway to the main station hub where Jack had to jump on the trolley. This time he wasn't a moment too late, but rather early. And after waiting twenty minutes for the right trolley, it was still long ride to the right station.

Jack took the spare key she had given him out of his pocket and slid it into the lock. The place seemed the same from the outside but he knew her family was going to be removing her things over the next week or so. Hopefully they hadn't started packing her into cardboard boxes. Not when she wanted him to watch something.

Opening the door, it was easy to see nothing had changed. A large pile of ignored mail was sitting on her dining table. Her ever tidy mother probably moved it from behind the front door when they arrived a couple days before the funeral. The plan had been for them to stay at Ava's place, but it was too hard on her parents. Just being here without her was hard enough for Jack.

It took him a moment to get his bearings in her place. Her family had managed to sort her into different piles of what they'd keep, what part to donate and what part of Ava they wanted to throw out. He didn't blame them for wanting to be rid of her memory. This last one wasn't the fondest one to be left with and dividing up her things was just part of the process.

In her spare bedroom, he found the VCR player laying haphazardly on its side in what could only be the trash pile. It made no sense to take the thing or donate the aging technology, no matter how great it worked. But it was going to serve a purpose now and later at his place. Like Ava, he too had an affinity for the ancient ways.

The television was hidden in the small remnants that were to be taken with her family. It was a fairly new TV and if nothing else could be sold on a rummage sale. Jack had discovered it behind a few taped boxes and under some blankets. He hauled over the set to where the connection in the wall was and attached the VCR cables.

The tape may have said *Election-Congressman S. Whitmore*, but that didn't make the idea of watching it any easier. What if it was mislabeled to avoid attention? Or something ghastly? But the second was out of the question for Ava and the first seemed unlikely. She had been fairly straightforward so far, albeit in riddles but straightforward nonetheless.

Jack slide the VHS cassette into the machine and flipped to the right input on the TV to watch it. It took a couple long, antagonizing minutes for the screen to jump to life with what was on the tape. It was nothing but an interview with the congressman recorded. Images of Samuel Whitmore flashed on the screen as a petite woman in a red suit discussed his background and introduced the man on stage with her.

Samuel Whitmore had been a conservative candidate in the election that year. Which made it seem even more unlikely that Ava thought he missed something. Jack had actually followed Whitmore for most of the campaign but had ultimately voted for the better candidate, his opponent. Not that Whitmore didn't have enough backing without his vote to take the seat. It seemed like a trivial issue of morals being misaligned with his own, but that could hardly be what Ava was after. Jack listened to the interview and it seemed to be the standard questions every politician was asked. But then it cut away halfway into the interview.

For a few seconds, there was nothing but the static and digital snow on the screen. Jack reached to shut off the machine but stopped when another clip came on. By the source name in the corner, it was a video from one of the big video sharing sites on the internet. It was shocking to think that somehow Ava had managed to jump ahead technologically to his level.

He watched the clip as best as he could after that revelation. There was a small statement that didn't seem to jive with what the congressman stood for. It was probably just a slip of tongue but then the congressman stopped the taping. It was followed by another sound byte to replace what he had let slip. The second version was what was mass released and what Jack had seen on the news. A rumor had surfaced about the first half of that clip, but was dismissed as being a tabloid rouse to disprove him.

When the clip cut out like the first one, there was no snow but the background of his computer. Somehow she had recorded the clip off his home computer to this tape. He lacked the right equipment which had to mean that she brought her VCR. On a couple occasions, she had done just that and they spent the night watching old movies. Normally she left around 10:00pm and there was no chance for her to record anything off his computer. But there was one time where it had gotten late and he refused to let her suffer by finding her way home on SEPTA, the public transportation. That was the only chance she'd have and it had to be after he fell asleep.

Jack glanced at the time in the corner. It was nearly two in the morning when this was recorded. That had to be when she added this to the tape. He sat there for a moment stumped. He waited for his computer background to flash out and be replaced by another clip, but it wasn't. Instead, he noticed the mouse on his computer slowly move to his start menu and open up a new document in Microsoft Word. Ava saved the file with the name <ATIS Chair Options>. It was something that Jack would have overlooked and that wasn't part of that project. But at the same time would draw attention that it didn't quite belong there.

It was a project he had finished months ago that he probably wouldn't have revisited. Until now that is. Jack paused the tape, in case there was yet more Ava was going to reveal. He went to get up to boot his computer before realizing where he was. *Shock that you got me all flustered again, Ava.* He sighed as he sat down; making a mental note to look for the file once he got back home.

Jack hit played and waited for the rest of the video to play. Maybe Ava was going to show him what was saved in that file now by typing it out. But the screen just turned into static and noise. He let it play out, thinking there'd be another clip. But five minutes later and a budding headache, Jack turned off the machine. He sat there in silence for a while before replacing the television where he found it and taking the VCR with him. Jack locked the door behind him and went to call a taxi. He wasn't going to be able to wait to read that file.

Chapter Eight

Inspector John Dunn paced the break room nervously. By some lucky star, the girl had committed suicide and taken a load off their shoulders. Ever since it came to Dunn's attention that this girl posed to reveal the biggest cover-up ever to break news in the past twenty years, it was wearing down on his sanity. Especially when the responsibility fell on him.

He knew it was a stupid delusion to think that she'd die in a wonderfully non-incriminating way. The only hassle was quickly covering up the incident when it occurred. Of course, there were plans of how best to deal with her disappearance. It happened that she was placed under surveillance a couple weeks before her death, but it had nothing to do with what she knew at this point. It was just to track her movements and make sure she didn't do anything stupid to compromise their operation. The only hiccup was separating her from the relationship she slipped into with one of the employees upstairs. It would be him that would cause the most commotion over her random disappearance.

The plan had been to orchestrate a conference that would only include herself and a few select members of the company. It would be moot to say that it would have only be a rouse to extract her from the office. The key to the plan had been to having one of her superiors deliver the invitation. Most of them would have shaken their heads at such a rouse and raised suspicion. The only other way to bring up the fake meeting was by eventually finding a peer who detested Koltrin enough not to care what happened to her. For all anyone knew, it would just be a prank or a surprise party for a possible promotion or her birthday. The motives behind it hadn't been ironed out completely, and now plans were no longer needed.

Dunn finally made his way back to his little office with a cup full of steaming coffee was in one hand. Right now should have been a time to relax but it hardly seemed that. As far as the general public knew, it was another suicide that had been cleaned up before the sight disturbed the public. A tiny blurb made its way into the newspaper about the death, withholding her name and listing it as merely "a trespasser". The company was pleased with the way it was handled and, those that knew and had been were nervous about the girl, were very relieved. Her family seemed to have accepted it and were nicely taking care of things with the little sympathy aid Amtrak extended.

The few loose ends would be easy enough to tie up now. One was the medical examiner's report that was conducted on what little remains were collected from the platform. Her sudden death had sparked interest to know exactly why she had done it. Was she on something or just unstable? Did someone else get to her and would they have to step in now to find the Good Samaritan? Luckily, the official report was sitting in a neat stack on his desk. It would make for some light reading, maybe even some enjoyment at knowing the last details of her life. Her last secrets.

The other loose end was much harder. *Jack Havest.* If he knew that her death was anything more than a suicide or that a plot was developed to eliminate his bed buddy, there was no doubt that Havest would sprout up with a dozen and a half questions. Aside from being the saddened lover, the only other problem was if Koltrin ever discussed anything with him on the subject. A secret like the one she had uncovered was one that was definitely worth killing over. It compromised every aspect of Amtrak's business operations with that great knowledge always came the temptation to release it.

The impression of their co-workers had been that there was a longstanding relationship between the two young employees. They have been observed eating lunch together numerous times after coming on their radar. The extent of their relationship could only be imagined, as to what occurred out of work. But with a long standing relationship that seemed to be functioning as not one, publically, and, with Havest being a man, it could only mean it was sustained by sex. It would be too much to hope that their relationship was strictly physical.

Jack Havest was a double threat. He could easily play the distraught lover just as easily as a confidante. He was as dangerous as when the girl had been alive. If that was the case, he would have to be dealt with quickly, after it was determined how much he knew. His death could easily be marked as depression at his loss and wanting to end his life to follow her into the hereafter.

Dunn rubbed his temple and took a sip of the coffee. After thirty years in uniform, both for the city of Philadelphia and Amtrak, this incident trumped drug busts, dog fighting rings, and the rare bomb threats that happened in the station. If so much wasn't riding on this, he'd retire this instant and be relaxing on a beach with a drink in his hand somewhere with his wife.

Instead, Inspector Dunn flipped open the file on top and skimmed over the cover sheet that inventoried what was taken from the scene. Again, it was nothing that varied from what he had handed over to the medical examiner nor was there anything personal on the list. He set that aside and reached from the toxicology portion of the report.

Chapter Nine

"John, we got a problem don't we?" Dunn glanced up as his right-hand man plopped down in the chair next to him. Marshall Thorpe had been his good buddy since they both joined the Amtrak force eight years ago. They had seen the good, the bad and the outright strange. But some mix of that was expected. Marshall had been there through thick and thin. That and he was a great guy to play a few hands of poker and knew his way around the golf course.

Dunn shook his head. "It doesn't make sense. The report from the medical examiner says there was nothing in her system at all."

"So she was just a crazy shit that jumped in front of a slow moving train? Never would have pegged her as a masochist." He smirked as he said it. Marshall never uttered a word, but Dunn knew him enough to know the thought of Ava had crossed his mind. He probably imagined doing things to her more after it was announced that she needed to disappear. And Marshall wouldn't object to that painful, and pleasuring, duty. No doubt he thought she'd enjoy some pain after putting up with that hopeless klutz of a romantic that was Havest.

"If she was crazy, why would the big shots go through this much trouble to shut her up? It would be easier to leak out information that she was unstable." He paused to take a drink. "The girl had a good head on her shoulders." Then again, he liked to think he did too. Just that sometimes his morals didn't like to line up with the paycheck, and this job was going to certainly pay off once things settled down.

"The only thing is that she purposely wanted to be seen. The video surveillance makes that clear. She's in every camera in the area, plus talking to as many of the bystanders in the concourse before slipping down the back stairs." *The girl knew she had to be remembered, and in a positive light too.* "She also made sure to jump so she'd be pinned in the four inch gap between the side of the train and platform. Luckily for us, she wasn't one of those that were conscious enough to still be alive and talking."

That would have been the worst – having a dying girl spill everything in her last moments of life to the passengers exiting the train. There was nothing that would have silenced her. No threat they could have issued. She would have died moments later anyways. Luckily, Ava Koltrin wasn't as crafty as she thought she was and those people in the station she talked to had disappeared before anyone was the wiser.

Chapter Ten

The taxi ride took only a quarter of the time it had taken Jack to get to Ava's place using SEPTA. Jack quickly paid the driver and dashed into his apartment. He didn't even bother to turn on a light, and instead let his memory of the layout guide him to his desk. Once there, it took only a minute for his computer to boot up. Then he followed the same motions Ava had showed him on the tape.

Sure enough, there was a file with the exact name hidden amongst the other ones in his project folder. He opened it, finding pages of text and images where the video clip must have left off. He skimmed the images that were first in the document and the comments Ava left for him.

It came to over twenty pages of pure text. It read like a bone dry non-fiction book, and the worst possible at that. As he began to read, he noticed what had to be Ava's comments in brackets scattered throughout. Then there were highlighted parts. Those struck him even more with just the content. Some of the bright yellow colored words mirrored what the VHS tape clips hinted at, and then went into further detail.

He read through the document until his cell went off. The caller ID told him it was his parents, yet again. They could wait for the three word reply. Jack had just gotten to more interesting, and incriminating, parts. The sources were perfectly listed, just to be through, and to make these accusations believable. He couldn't resist checking some of them himself. It was engrossing material. So much so that it was growing dark outside and even his stomach couldn't pry his eyes away from the screen. But one thing seemed to shatter his thoughts.

Jack paused as he heard the chimes from the center of town.

Chapter Eleven

Ava walked alongside him. Her mitten hand in his gloved one. It was the first snowfall since they'd return to Philly from visiting Ava's family in Texas. It had been like a whole different country down there. And if Jack had been thinking straight, they wouldn't have come back to their jobs and stayed in the south all winter.

But she had made sure they'd be back for some part of winter. At the first flakes falling, she had wrapped his scarf around his neck and tugged his reluctant body into his jacket. Once he was pried from the comfortable futon, and agreed to wander into the cold, only then did she bundle up herself.

It wasn't a terribly cold day by any standard, but Jack preferred the warm summer months and the hot rays on his skin. Ava knew this and sometimes he wondered if she wasn't just torturing him. But he had to laugh at the thought of his little Ava torturing him to any measure. If anything it was the other way around.

They left his apartment and walked down the freshly covered sidewalk. The fresh powder leaving two solitary lines of footprints. It felt as if they were the only two people in the world. And right now, to each other, they were.

They walked towards the little park in the center of Narberth, Pennsylvania. It was a small, yet charming, town that seemed to gain a special sparkle during the winter holiday season. A Christmas tree had replaced the fountain in the center of the park. It was already alit tonight, three weeks before Christmas. Just a few days before her death. They had been happy in the falling snow.

They had made it to the Christmas tree just as the bells chimed the top of the hour. Jack had glanced over at her, seeing her gazing at the snowflakes as they fell on the lights and ornaments. He had gently squeezed her hand as he moved in front of her.

"I'm going to hang mistletoe all over our places to get back at you for dragging me out in the cold to watch snow fall." Jack smiled as he pulled her closer. "But I love you like crazy, Ava."

They had kissed as the bells continued to chime eight times. Small flakes that fell melted as they landed on their faces, going largely unnoticed. He had felt a smile slowly grow on Ava's face.

"Well, I always knew you were crazy to fall in love with me."

Chapter Twelve

It was one of those happier times that he'd truly miss now that she was gone. The holidays were going to be harder. His family seemed to have warned him of that, but it was one thing to say it and another to actually feel it... and now he was feeling it.

The chimes had stopped, but there was light snow falling outside his window now. Ava had always teased him that he was too much of a pansy to enjoy the snowy winter. She knew it was because he didn't care for being cold; it was just playfully teasing between them. There were things he teased her about. Like how she must be part polar bear after being born and raised in the upper peninsula of Michigan. She was a Yooper, and proud of it. This was before her parents had moved south after their children left the nest.

Jack got up from his computer desk and headed over to his closet. "Ava, you better be watching me from wherever you are and seeing this." He slipped into his winter boots and pulled on his jacket. The last thing he did before slipping outside into the snow was to wrap his favorite scarf around his neck. He wasn't sure what he was really going to do. Ava would have sneaked behind him and threw a couple snowballs at him before laughing and running off, so as not to be caught and tossed in a snow bank. That kind of fun was hard with only one.

He sighed as he gave into just taking a long walk. Maybe that would be enough to make her smile at his attempt to survive the wintry weather from where she was now. The thought made him smile for a moment. The snow had gently covered an icy spot that lay just underneath on the path he had chosen. And, of course, now he was laying on his back staring up at the flakes plummeting down towards him after falling backwards in slow motion.

Instead of complaining and grumbling, he chuckled to himself. "You got me again, Ava." He sighed, taking mental inventory. Nothing seemed broken, but tomorrow there were going to be bruises and a lot of soreness. "But you know you could have gone easier on me."

"Are you alright, mister?" Jack turned to see a little face staring at him. A small boy was crouched, looking at him. "I can get my mommy. She kisses my boo-boos and makes them feel better."

Jack sat up and smiled at the kid. He was enjoying his snow excursion too much to realize that it wasn't going to be possible to have children with Ava, like he had hoped would happen one day. No little smiling faces looking up at him like this little boy's.

"No, I'm fine. See?" He moved his arms and legs. It seemed to reassure the lad that this stranger wasn't terribly hurt. Well, other than maybe his pride and hindquarters.

The boy giggled before plopping down in the snow next to him. He just watched the boy wiggle around in the snow. After a few minutes, the boy stopped and sat up. "I made one too."

Jack looked around the smiling boy to see a little snow angel. Glancing around himself, he just saw the outline from when he fell. The boy must have thought he was making snow angels, seeing how he said he was fine. Jack's falling could be credited to the artistic flare on execution, and telling the boy otherwise would probably crush the fun they seemed to be having.

"Look at that. You did, kid, and what an awesome snow angel it is too!" Jack smiled and laughed lightly. He could only imagine how silly the two of them looked in the middle of the sidewalk making snow angels.

He grabbed a handful of snow and fashioned it into a lopsided snowball. "Have you ever tossed snowballs, kid?" Jack lobbed the ball at one of the trees along the snowy sidewalk.

The boy shook his head. His mother probably taught him not to throw snowballs and Jack was going to mess the kid up. He watched as the two little mitten hands squished together fluffy white snow. The boy threw the snowball at the tree but it dissolved into small pieces midair. "My name's Mikey. You don't have to keep calling me kid."

Mikey tried again as he watched Jack make another snowball. They had both missed the first time, but the second time fared better for one of them at least. Mikey's nicked the side of the tree while Jack missed completely again.

"Try again." Mikey handed him a small ball of fluff that he made. "My mommy says don't never give up, even when things are bad. Because then they stay bad and you can't make them better. She also says that everything gets better in time and there are silver linens."

Jack laughed as he took the snowball from his new little buddy. "I think you mean a silver lining not linen. Linens are things like towels and bed sheets." He looked at the little ball before throwing it at the tree. This time there was a white blob on the bark where it hit. He stared at the blob, thinking about the wise words Mikey had just told him.

"You know, your mother's right." He said finally, getting up and dusting the snow off. Just a pathetic snow angel remained on the sidewalk to mark his presence. That's just what Jack had to do, and maybe that was Ava's plan all along. Maybe that's why she was going through the trouble of leaving him these breadcrumbs. She had promised he'd be happy with either choice, and Jack knew that she'd make sure that, no matter what, there'd be a smile on his face. It was just who she was.

"It was nice to meet you, Mikey. I just remembered something I have to do." He started to head back home before stopping a few feet away. "Your mother's a smart lady. Listen to her, okay?" He turned to head back to his apartment, and the daunting file on his computer.

Chapter Thirteen

Dunn had gone out for a few beers after work with a few friends. He needed a drink or two after the day he had. It had started off as a good day with Koltrin tying up most of the loose ends, but it was the fact that they'd have to go after Jack Havest now that was the problem. And the reason for his alcoholic excursion.

To find out if he was a threat, they'd have to confront him. Doing that would only tip him off. The small public investigation was basically over. The reports and news clippings were done. It was almost old news, buried and forgotten. Poking around would only put the man on alert of the scandal they were covering up.

John plopped down on his living room couch. Down the hall, he could faintly hear his wife snoring. He had called home to tell her he was going out so she wouldn't worry. It wasn't unusually to go out with his buddies. It was if he went out alone that she'd have to be concerned. That was the only time his alcohol level rose far too high and everything got out of control.

He had tucked the medical report in his bag. One thing John wanted to do was keep work and his personal life separate, but the file was a little too hefty and his curiosity got the best of him. Knowing his wife wouldn't be interrupting his thoughts and clandestine activity, he pulled it from his satchel.

Most of it was the boring stuff and John had suffered through that earlier during the day. There were just a few sections that he wanted to reread and a couple that he hadn't yet got to read. To his dismay, the sections he hoped would give him the most pleasure only disappointed.

Koltrin hadn't taken anything prior to her stunt. Nor had she eat ate, not that her choice of last meal would have had an impact on anything. There weren't any substances in her system, not even a trace of caffeine. Nothing could be pinned on her, unlike what the false reports and clippings spun out. She was just a normal girl, in every way. She didn't divulge in risqué behaviors no tattoos or piercings in hidden venues. And to further ruin his illusions and buzz, he learned there was enough evidence to strongly suggest she was pregnant. Not quite a month by what the coroner could determine. But that would be another stone in his boot if it ever got out.

It seemed like nothing he thought was right. Nothing about this girl was particularly interesting or dangerous, other than she had acquired some knowledge that could tear the company apart. But after memorizing Ava Koltrin's life story through this investigation, he couldn't figure out how or what she learned that was worth killing over. A person in her position would never have access to anything of value. But apparently, Ava Koltrin had found out the wrong things about Amtrak.

Chapter Fourteen

Jack had gone over the file and the video so many times that he could almost quote it word for word. His apartment thusly was littered with a week's worth of take-out containers, empty pop cans and bags of chips. Every moment that he wasn't at work was spent on this. And what made things worse was this was a dead end.

With the other breadcrumbs, Ava had led him to the next clue. But this time, the video ran to the end of the tape showing nothing but static. He also ran a fine toothed comb through the file for a hidden note. But no matter how many times he searched, nothing was found that he could go on with.

He paced the worn route between his desk and television. His thoughts had taken over so much so that when his cell phone vibrated, he jumped three feet in the air. It scared the life out of him. Angered, he pulled the device out of his pocket. It had to be his family again checking up on him. He was about to call them to tell them for the millionth time he was fine when he looked at the caller ID.

Jack froze, even when he felt the phone slip from his hand and heard it hit the floor. *It wasn't possible.* There was no way she sent it. He sat on the floor and picked up the cell. There was no doubt that it said 'Ava Koltrin' and the number was her cell. *But Ava was dead!* He knew there was no way she could have sent it to him. But at the same time, his mind humored the idea she was alive somewhere, somehow.

Chapter Fifteen

Jack sat in silence debated whether or not to open the text. In the end, his curiosity got the better of him. To his disappointment, it wasn't her and the text said so.

'I was paid weeks ago to send you this text today if the package left for you wasn't returned. I don't really know Ava but agreed to do as she asked. She said it was important.'

His disappointment read clearly on his face. The hope that she might still be alive somewhere was crushed. He should have known better. He knew how she died and had suffered through her funeral. Ava would have never put him through that if she was alive somewhere else.

'She wants you to go here:
www.sawasdee_ka.azure.com.'

Jack looked at the web address. He only recognized half of it. "Ava, what in the world is on this site?"

The date of the site's creation was posted at the top of the splash page. The only thing was the name of the site, *Sawasdee Ka ~Ava*, and its translation *Hello ~Ava*.

Jack had no idea what language the greeting was in, but it didn't surprise him knowing Ava's interest in linguistics. But this was hardly what she wanted to tell him. He ran the computer mouse over the otherwise empty page until he found a hidden link. She had made sure the color of the link was the exact same as the background until a cursor rolled over it.

'Welcome Jack.'

Chapter Sixteen

Welcome Jack... I hope you weren't too crushed to find I'm still very much dead, or will be very much dead by the time you read this. This website's just for you to read and to remember the good old days. Most of what's here is stuff I NEED to say even though you'll probably say you know it already. There are a few links at the bottom to photos I took, some of our songs, and a few of our instant message conversations. I hope you're not too mad at me for keeping them. I didn't want to forget and end up finding out you were just a dream.

~Ava

Jack stared at the page, a little in daze. He was curious as to what exactly she kept from their relationship. He could only imagine as the cursor hovered over the instant message link and then over the link to the photos. But instead he decided to wait and hit the <Next> button. And with that, another entry came up on the screen to replace the previous one.

I know you're wondering why I would even think about killing myself. But there were things I never told you and I regret holding stuff back from you. I just never thought you'd understand like I hoped and I didn't want to burden you. The last thing I wanted was to scare you away or get those looks of pity. Even if you didn't, I'd always feel like there was something between us and imagine things reflecting in your eyes.

You knew my past was a troubling one, but I could never tell you. My childhood was taken from me by my parents who needed a "perfect" daughter. They had the perfect jock son and fell into the delusion of the ideal family. I was forced to play their games and lost myself. For 18 years, the real me was hidden behind all their smoke and mirrors. And every single day I thought about ending my life, even planned it 'til after my body was cold in the earth and the stone I wanted on my grave.

But I survived that dark life and made it past the suicide to recreate my life. When I met you, it was only the second year of recovering myself. At first, all I wanted to do was push you away like I had anyone I even remotely cared for. You never fit the perfect image my family had, but I saw you and you fit my perfect image. And I love you for who you are and not who you were trying to be. And I love you for who you make me, simply by being around you.

We talked about everything and anything we could, but I could never feel worthy of the time spent with you. It always felt like I was holding you back and wasting your time. Never once did you say anything to make me think that. In fact, you very much so did the opposite. But I couldn't shake my past and I know it pulled at us. You're going to get annoyed at me saying this, but I am sorry for that.

I want to give you one last chance to bail now, Jack. I'll stop sending you tidbits that will lead you to what really happened and why I was on the platform waiting for you. So that I'm clear... if you stay with me a little longer, I will tell you what I apparently couldn't and I will try to heal your heart. If you want to leave, I understand. You just need to go to the splash page and click the welcome message while holding Alt + P. That will delete the page and tell my messenger to stop. The choice is yours. It has always been yours, Jack. And no matter what, I still love you.

Yours Forever,
Ava

Chapter Seventeen

Dunn watched from outside his favorite coffee place in the station as Jack Havest walked by. He looked a complete mess and suffering as he waited in line for his cup of sugar and caffeine. It amused the inspector, watching the haggard man take a few slow sips of his steaming brew.

Ava's death was a while ago now and, having been observing the only loose end, Havest's appearance today was off-the-books shocking. His hair was uncombed. His beard unkempt. And his clothes looked slept in. Dunn expected this of the man right after her death, not now. He doubted Havest's work was the reason for his current appearance. With no work interference or any personal life, the only idea Dunn could deduce was that he was looking into something secretive. And it could very well be Koltrin's death.

"Someone's falling to pieces. Guess this was what he was like before the girl." Marshall Thorpe sat down with a poppy seed muffin and a large coffee. "Wonder why a girl like *that* would bother with a mess like *this*. I wonder if she got a kick out of charity cases. I can only imagine the charity she gave that boy."

Dunn could hear the sullen tone in his partner's voice. He could tell Thorpe thought that Havest had never done any of the fantasies he had imagined Ava being into. They had shared many laughs at his expense, but Dunn wasn't going to put himself through more torture of listening to all the erotic things Thorpe would do to the 'inexperienced with satisfaction' lover.

"Looks like he can't even dress himself without his mommy." A deep laugh came from the other side of the table as Havest walked by and disappeared into the elevator to the offices above. Dunn had seen what had made his partner laugh so hard. To add to the peculiar appearance, Jack Havest was wearing two very different socks in untied shoes.

"Cut it out, Marshall. Finish your muffin so we can get going. I have to get ready for lunch, which means finishing the report."

Chapter Eighteen

Dunn sat in his office with the door closed. It had taken a couple hours, but he had finally gotten rid of Thorpe. Usually the man was good company, but he was getting annoyed with hearing nothing but 'Havest this...' and 'Havest that...' There was no normal talk about the game last night or latest politician's rant that was to be expected from his companion. Besides, Dunn wanted to focus on the file in his hands.

It was just the beginning of March and only a few months since the girl was cold in the ground. Havest had seemed to have moved on until this morning. It was just further proof that something needed to be done with him. It was something Dunn should probably have done from the start. They got rid of one person, what would one more be? It could have been a lover's quarrel gone wrong, a murder-suicide, or something of that nature.

But this file wasn't on Ava Koltrin. It was on Jack Havest. From the moment the company heard of the man, up until an hour ago when the security camera caught him coming out of the elevator to get another coffee and a banana, his appearance had seemed more normal. It was probably the result of a scared co-worker saying something and a long, fruitless, fight with a comb.

Dunn knew talking to the guy was unavoidable, but today seemed like a good enough day as any. That and with Havest's change in appearance, it wouldn't be a hard segway into talking about the girl and what he's up to. Bringing her up that way wouldn't seem too obvious that he had alternative motives. Dunn might actually seem sympathetic to the lad. And this way the poor sap wouldn't suspect he was being interrogated.

The file read like a very bland amateur-written novel, if it could be called that. It seemed to consist of a list of dates and major information, such as his start date and any promotions or big projects he worked on. Then there were old transcripts from his university and a small portfolio of school work that was relevant to his current work, or so Dunn waged a guess. And unless the Havest wandering around somewhere in the building was an imposter, the stack of references and recommendation letters told a different story. One past employer talked about his professionalism and interpersonal skills. Another highlighted his demeanor and integrity. He had to wonder what these people would say if they say Havest today in all his glory.

There didn't seem to be much interesting information on the man. There were just two uninteresting, meddle-some people who threatened his retirement plans; however, that was their downfall last time. They hadn't expected Koltrin to be anything more than a programmed office drone. She had taught them a lesson that they weren't going to forget any time soon.

Dunn straightened up the files and placed them nicely back into the manila folder. The most secure place in the small office was the little floor mounted safe under his desk that was always kept under lock and key. He hid the folder before locking the safe and then locking the office door as he left. There shouldn't be anyone snooping around his office nor anyone that would have a reason to be here or know what was being kept. Then again, there was no policy against the police department keeping employee records in their offices. If anyone accused him of anything suspicious, Dunn could claim to be looking into a complaint or a tip and slip in a fake document to back himself up.

He headed out into the food court to see if he could spot the walking mess. Usually the two had chosen a table nearer to the windows but, since Koltrin's death, Havest had completely changed up the seating choices. He instead headed for the edges of the table area and stuck to himself. And that was just how he found him today.

Dunn quickly picked up something from one of the food places in the station. He noticed how much his target had left to eat, but that wasn't a good determination of the time range he had left to strike up a conversation. When Dunn had lost a close buddy to a fishing boat accident years ago, he couldn't stomach food and had no desire to attempt it. The only thing was that Havest had gotten over her death and now had slipped back into a slump.

"Mind if I join you, Jack?"

Chapter Nineteen

Jack looked up to see an older uniformed man. It was going to be hard to explain why he would decline the company. It wasn't like he could say that Ava was tormenting him slowly with this crazy half-baked scheme of hers. And from all the secrets and hidden messages, he knew nothing of what Ava wanted him to know. Besides if what Ava knew had killed her, she would have gone to the police if it was safe. With her still dying, they might not have been able to protect her from whatever she had fallen into.

He shrugged and watched as the man sat across from him. "I'm Inspector John Dunn. I was one of the Amtrak officers that responded when Ms. Koltrin died."

Jack had a hard time registering this odd conversation. Already, it seemed out of the ordinary. Then again, he had just caught a glimpse of himself in the mirror and had to tidy up, before he noticed the mismatching socks on his way down, and pulled off both socks. At least his feet matched; well, the last time he checked at least.

"I couldn't help but notice what a mess you looked like this morning. But while I didn't really know her, I saw her right before she died. I thought it might help if you had someone to talk to about it. Maybe you're not completely over her or are having trouble moving on."

He wasn't sure why the inspector was telling him all this. It wasn't making him feel better. And in no way did he think the man across from him was on a delusional witch hunt or trying to toy even more with his mind.

"I know you were extremely close, and you probably never heard all the details. And seeing how you are, maybe that's why you can't move on. It happened with me with my fishing buddy." Dunn took slow breaths as he wondered how to proceed.

"She didn't make it in front of the engine. She missed beating the train into the station and got caught between the train and the platform. In those four inches, her body spun as the train rolled in, pinning her in that small gap when it finally stopped. Like a few of the unfortunate ones, she was still alive but barely conscious."

Jack could picture it all in his mind, in all its gruesome glory. It wasn't common but he had heard a similar story years ago when he joined up with the railroad. His stomach was slightly protesting, but he couldn't stop his curiosity from wanting to know every detail about Ava.

"We had migrated the passengers away from where she was, so they never saw anything. Usually we tilt the car with a jack and pull the person out. Because they spin and get caught in such a small space, their body is basically in two and barely connected by their spine or strips of flesh. Ava died before we could move the car.

And when we did, we saw her body had completely separated and she bled to death where her body pinched into two, just below her bust line"

Jack was feeling sick; more so than when he heard she died or when the notes from beyond the grave started. It wasn't so much the images of a gruesome death. He knew suicides and deaths caused by trains weren't pretty, no matter who was at fault. But he had hoped that somehow it wasn't painful for her. That maybe she was high or drunk and she was ran over versus being twisted until she snapped in two.

"I'm sorry, boy. I didn't mean to make you ill." He felt a cool hand on his own. "Take a deep breath. It'll pass."

"Th-thanks for telling me how she died." Jack said quietly.

He really wasn't thankful at all. It was worse knowing she had suffered now. He couldn't help but wonder, even more, why she did it. She must have gone to the police. And why didn't they help her? Someone should have stopped her. He should have been there to stop her.

"Did you know any of that or hear any other stories? People up in the offices like to exaggerate and make things up."

Jack shook his head, only making matters worse. His brain felt like goo being sloshed around in his skull.

"Do you know why she jumped? Anything she might have mentioned to you that seemed out of the ordinary. It might help, even if it doesn't seem like it was important." The inspector tried to probe, but Jack wasn't able to focus anymore. Just thoughts of her bloody, torn body filled his head.

"I don't know. She would never kill herself." His speech was slow as he tried to process his jumbled thoughts into sentences before letting them out of his mouth. "There wasn't anything out of the ordinary. We barely talked the month before. We were apart for work; she had some project her boss was getting after her for, so we didn't talk much. I know she said she had to print the last of the project drawings about two nights before she died. It was the last time she called and she had cut out when a storm took out the cell towers."

He had remembered that night because it was late for her to be calling. The change in time zones had also added to the difficulty of talking. Plus, she had worked night shifts a few times during their period apart too. Jack was thrilled when she called and they both had a chance to talk. Ava had said she had something important to tell him, but then the storm wiped out the cell towers and their call was cut short. He had tried for an hour to call her back but couldn't get through.

"I... I have to get back to work. Big deadline." Jack excused himself, throwing away his lunch as he left.

Lunch had turned out to be a disappointment for the inspector. He had made his intended target ill instead of guilty or spewing out information. Although Havest was probably spewing stuff out now, but nothing too pleasant or helpful in Dunn's eyes.

Chapter Twenty

Dunn retreated to his office at the end of his shift. He learned little from Havest. It seemed as if the girl hadn't told him anything. She promised she wouldn't. Begged for Havest's life over her own, once it was clear that they didn't trust her to be silent. After all, what was one more body?

"I'm way too old for this." He moaned as he sat down in his seat to write out his thoughts on the lunch meeting. There really wasn't much to scribble down. Things like what he attempted to eat or what he wore were insignificant details. All Dunn could touch on were how Havest reacted to the sudden company and how his behavior was during the meal. He was relatively calm, for sitting with someone interrogating him. The years of training seemed to confirm that Havest knew nothing, or was a sociopath.

But now he needed a plan on how to deal with the boy. The bigger question was whether anything needed to be done at all. He had no knowledge and as far as Dunn could decipher from the personnel file, he was an asset to the company's longevity. He wanted his monthly checks to keep coming once he retired, so a belly-up company wouldn't fit that bill.

Dunn moved further down the page to write his suggestions for further action. He'd monitor the boy and gather information. Any hint of suspicion or wayward action, then he would react. It was hard to personally justify extra action to take that would cost the boy his life or career. That, and maybe, because it was the girl's only request – to keep him alive. It was his call and, right about now, he was ready to be over with it. The whole thing was wrapped up like a nice present under the tree at Christmas.

Chapter Twenty-One

Jack plopped down on this futon. It had been a rough day after lunch. He accomplished nothing. Well, other than completely emptying his stomach. Jack had grabbed a cold, dampened towel out of the bathroom and laid it over his face. There was a little relief from it, but it couldn't get the gory thoughts out of his head.

All because that cop decided he needed to tell him how she died. Which wasn't completely what their little announcement about her death said. If she was high or drunk, she probably would have fallen or stumbled into the path of the train, not jumped. And it was odd that he wanted to know if she said anything strange. When Jack replied that she never mentioned suicide, the inspector still seemed to be waiting for a different answer. Why would he be searching for an answer to why she died when he already knew?

Jack pulled himself off the futon, leaving the towel on the coffee table. Ava hadn't sent the next clue yet. Maybe he had overlooked it. She had hidden a link within the secret site for him. Maybe she had hid the next clue as well.

He systematically went through her keepsakes. The conversations were painful. He had heard her voice saying every word she once typed to him, but there was nothing. Then, he listened to every song. Twice. No secret meanings or clues that he could figure out. Jack knew it had to be simple. Ava knew he wasn't the brightest star in the sky sometimes.

"Ava, if you weren't dead, I'd strangle you!" Every file he went through only made him more frustrated and feel at a lost. He couldn't fail her now. Maybe if he hadn't failed to listen before or maybe, somehow, had been able to stop her that day on the platform that she'd be sitting next to him laughing at his failed attempts to crack her code.

The photos were separated. One was personal, which contained photos of them and their families, and the other was work related, sites she'd been to and project's she worked on. There was nothing that really stuck out to him in the personal photos except how badly he had needed a haircut when they were taken. That and how she managed to only post the ones where he looked like a complete dork or baboon.

This was the last place that he had to search. There were no secrets in the other clues. Those he had already taken under a microscope. Jack clicked through the photos again. He managed a laugh. He *did* look like a complete dork but compared to his appearance earlier today, he'd take dork over that. He concentrated more on the faces in the photos, seeing as nothing stood out. Maybe someone else had a worse hair day than he had.

He realized that most of the photos had track gangs that he had worked with when he was out in the field. Sometimes he greatly missed their antics; but then again, sometimes they were too rambunctious and like evil little kids. Maybe it was supervising those gangs that made him unwilling to have children of his own. Jack knew he didn't have the stamina for that. But after meeting Ava, his thoughts were changed a little. It wasn't like he'd be doing it alone, and Ava would have made an awesome mother. He sighed and was about to shut off the computer for the night, tired of living in the 'what if' moments.

"Ava never brought a camera to work," he mumbled to himself, the mouse hovering over the shutdown button. The personal photos didn't have many with her in them and the ones she were in, they had asked someone to take their photo. The work ones all had her in them. It almost seemed that she was the focus of the picture. Very few had her looking at the camera, as if these were taken without her knowing. But she had saved them for him.

Jack moved closer to the screen. Ava's little pixilated self-revealed nothing more up closer, but he did notice a police officer reoccurring in the photos. In most of them, he appeared to be watching Ava or talking in her general direction. It wasn't much in the way of a clue. It didn't make sense that Amtrak police would single her out at a work site. Then again, it wasn't common for them to come to the types of projects where the photos were taken.

The officer didn't look familiar. Jack pasted the photo into the computer's image editing program and cropped it. The face was blurred a bit but it was something. He hit the print button and retrieved the paper from his printer down the hall in the room set up as a mini office. Tomorrow he'd look for the man at 30th Street Station. Maybe, by some chance, he worked in the station.

Maybe the police force was up to something. Ava had somehow gotten a hold of photos that showed them doing something out of the ordinary. Another thing out of the ordinary was Inspector Dunn consoling him at lunch; if that's what his questioning could be called.

Dunn interrogated me!

He couldn't believe it took him this long to catch on. It was suspicious but at the time his feelings and stomach were getting the better of him. It seemed to give more proof that police were up to something and Ava most likely didn't go to them with whatever information she knew.

It felt good to have something to go on again. Ava probably hadn't expected he'd make that out on his own. She seemed to be the overprotective one and, for the longest time, it felt like she didn't think he could do anything on his own. Ava wasn't an easy one to figure out but luckily she was straightforward and honest. That was the only way he would have figured that out. Their openness and communication was what got them through things like that and kept them together for so long. He smiled and shoved the trophy into his jacket pocket so he wouldn't forget it. It would be classic Jack to have this little victory and then to lose what he had worked so hard to get. And he couldn't let Ava laughed at him over this after his little goofy victory dance.

Thinking of her laughter was both uplifting and depressing. He missed it terribly now, but the idea that he had made her laugh one more time was worth his humiliation. He logged off the computer and headed down the hall to do something he hadn't on his own for a long time. He was going to try to cook something and not burn the place down.

Chapter Twenty-Two

Ava flopped on her bed, burying her face into the pillow. It felt like her heart was ripped out of her chest. Everything was being slowly taken from her and there was nothing she could do about it. It was taking all her will power not to tell Jack. He was an amazing boyfriend, but she couldn't burden him with the load she had to carry. Being a burden was the last thing Ava ever wanted to be. She had decided long ago to never tell him.

The secret she learned was by pure accident. Of course, she had always been an ear for anyone who needed to just talk and get things out. Ava was an ear, whether she wanted to be or not, and different things had come to pass onto her. Within her first few months at Amtrak, she had learned things by word of mouth that people having worked there for years didn't even know. It made her more valuable but, at the same time, it was more dangerous for her to know things above her pay grade. That was all how she felt. It was always secrets and lies. What was worse was she had to keep it from the man she loved to protect him from her fate.

Tears were pouring down her face, drenching the pillow she clutched. It wasn't the secrets or knowing she might be hurting Jack by keeping something from him. It was all from knowing she had to let him go to save him. The only way he'd stay alive and sane was if she broke them up. It was killing her to think about being apart from him though.

He was her perfect missing half, her soul mate. Their personalities were different but they worked together. Even though she had a hard, crappy past, he had made it better just by being himself. Somehow he had healed her, though he'd never know and she'd admit it. She was a better person because of him. He had stolen her heart and she promised herself never to let anything hurt him. Now she was going to do the one thing that would kill him... and it was killing her.

Chapter Twenty-Three

There had to be a way to fix everything. Things had gone too far. They were going to come for her. Their threats were hitting closer and closer to home. And they were getting desperate.

They began by asking, or rather telling her, to stop things and forget all she knew. Then they had followed her, at first, around the station and then out to her projects in the field. She had noticed and was able to find the pictures they took of her on a shared drive, but she had no idea why they had been taken. The police had stopped following her shortly after that and, even though she knew that, Ava was more paranoid than ever. She had doubled the security measures she took in the office and had a new safety system installed at her home. Nothing felt safe anymore, not even being wrapped in Jack's arms.

It was then that they began threatening Jack. She knew they were using her feelings against her. She loved him too much to let anything happen to him. So she decided to play their game. Maybe if they felt threatened, they would just back off or reach a stalemate. But they were fighting back. Was her word of silence not good enough for them anymore? They all knew that if she spoke Amtrak was over and a huge scandal would ensue. She would keep quiet if they promised not to touch Jack.

The police nulled the offer. Ava knew they wanted her dead. She could just leave the company; maybe she could even demand payment for her silence. But she couldn't leave the most important thing, person, in her life. For weeks, she tried to talk to Jack but he didn't seem to let her get a word in edgewise that would vary from their normal conversation. He even seemed to ignore her texts and emails that tried to bring it up. It was like his mind was focused on something else.

"I'm not going to be able to take him with me." She spoke softly through the tears. "If I'm going to kill him, I need to heal him and help him move on." It was a whisper now, but that was the only way she could end this.

That officer had made it clear what she had to do to protect Jack. She was going to have to keep silent *forever.* She was going to lose her love, but she could accept it if she could make sure Jack could be happy after she was gone. And Ava made a plan to help him do that. She wanted him to smile and laugh, and even find love again.

"Please let me do this for you, Jack. I love you and just want you to be happy. Don't fight me for a change and make my death worthless."

Chapter Twenty-Four

She sat downstairs, trying patiently to wait. Her outfit was perfectly matched from her lipstick-red blouse to her black houndstooth shoes. It was her first day as an engineering associate.

Ava had arrived an extra half hour early. There were a couple forms left before it was official and a few signatures were all that was needed to get the ID badge and start doing some good work. She had tried to call her boss, but there was no answer. She was left at the mercy of the human resource department in remembering she was coming and sending someone to fetch her.

"Ave Koltrin?" An older gentleman greeted her near the elevators to the offices above. "I'm Patrick Smith, head of business development. I recognized you from the ID badge photo that's sitting on my desk. Why don't we go upstairs and we'll get you started."

Two hours later, she found herself sitting with the Track Standards Engineer. He had a strange sense of humor that she was able to understand and dish back out. It was a bold move to joke with the higher ups, especially on the first day, but they were just people too. Well it seemed most of them were, if you ignored the crazy ones and those that worked instead of sleeping; but he seemed to be a decent fellow and she enjoyed the morning spent with him. From his stories, Ava had learned a lot about the company and the history of the railroad.

Lunch was rather boring, having spent it both alone and eating at a familiar restaurant chain in the station below. She had been promised more stories, in what seemed to be the only exciting part of her new job so far. But when Ava made it back upstairs, it seemed one of them had real work to be done, work that couldn't be delayed or put off with another story.

"Ava, I'm sorry but there's an issue with a stretch of welded rail. I got to head out there. If you had your gear, you might have been able to come along. But now you're going to have to…" He paused, his hand hovering over his cell phone. "Why don't I introduce you to someone?"

There was an odd smile on his face that sent up warnings. But given the morning's lack of agenda, it was probably just her co-worker's scheme to pass her off. She could only hope whoever the next person was as entertaining.

"Ava Koltrin, I'd like you to meet Jack Havest. Jack is our Engineer of Infrastructure Improvement." Jack laughed a little by his introduction.

"That's sounds a lot better than resident rail nerd. I'm working on extending the lifespan of our rail." He got up and shook Ava's hand. "It's a pleasure to meet you, Ava."

Chapter Twenty-Five

He walked through the station floor of 30th Street. Jack glanced at every officer that passed by and made his rounds around the mezzanine to make sure there wasn't one being missed.

Jack sat down on one of the long benches. He finally thought he had a clue to go on, but it had been a week and this daily ritual was taxing. He couldn't help thinking that this wasn't the clue Ava meant for him to find. It could have easily been a fabrication of his mind, wanting to see things that weren't there. She could have chosen those photos because they simply were candid shots of her like some strange photo scavenger hunt. *"And here we see an Ava in her natural habit. Observe how she scrutinizes the welded joint to ensure a smooth ride by the train sets that travel over it."*

He sighed and watched a group of passengers conversing with an older officer. Treves, if Jack recalled correctly. A seemingly nice man but, then again, if this was a police conspiracy that could mean nothing. Seeing the passengers gave him an idea. Jack pulled out the photo and walked over.

"Treves?" He asked and was pleased when the officer turned with a smile. So he had correctly remembered the man's name. Another thing that he'd rub in Ava's face if she was here. "I was wondering if you knew who this officer is."

Treves took the photo and glanced at it. "Could you have gotten a poorer photo?" Sure it was blurry, and a little grainy.

"Sorry, but it's the best I have." The man laughed and took a closer look.

"Looks like Paul Garfield."

Jack took the photo back. Finally, he had a name and a new lead. "Do you know where I can find him?"

"Paul died about a month ago from a heart attack. He didn't last long in retirement." The man glanced at a small group wandering around. "I need to get back to work but you could try his old partner."

Jack nodded. It was too much to hope that he could talk to Garfield but maybe this partner would know something about where the photo was taken or why.

"John Dunn. He's working this afternoon."

His face drained of blood. There was no way that he had just mentioned Dunn. It was impossible. The worst part was the fear building inside him now. Dunn had admitted he was there where Ava died. Dunn had interrogated him at lunch. Dunn was connected to the officer who seemed to be watching Ava, possibly the one to take the photo. What if Dunn had him in the crosshairs now? He might as well been the one to push Ava in front of that train. Her death was on him, as far as Jack was concerned.

He watched as Treves walked off with the group, aiding however he was asked. This was the last time that he could go to the police. That much was crystal clear. Jack had no idea what connections and relationships Dunn had with the other officers, and each person was a potential trap.

It felt like a dead end. The one thing he had managed to outsmart Ava on and now his victory was just a bigger failure. He needed to find something. He was desperate and his mind was reeling. There had to be something that he was overlooking. Jack tucked the photo into his pant pocket and headed back upstairs to the offices.

He made his way to Ava's cubicle. It felt almost painful to be in this section of the building again, even when it was so close to his own. It was just that Jack needed to find something. As careful as she was, he knew Ava probably had done some of that research or website from her work computer. That meant there could be more saved files and photos that were unused or not uploaded. Maybe that's why there wasn't another clue yet. Ava might have died before she could plan the next one out.

Jack heard typing as he rounded the corner and saw her replacement busy at work. Charles Dolfry didn't recognize him when Jack knocked on the wall, so not to startle the man this time. He needed information and Dolfry probably wouldn't help if he was rattled.

"Yes?" Not rattled, but slightly annoyed. Maybe there was hope.

"I was wondering if you knew what they did with Ava's computer. We were working together on a project and I realized that she had the preliminary work on hers. I need to grab the files for a presentation tomorrow." It was a lie but it sounded good. The only problem now would be if it was refreshed and reassigned to another employee. Then everything would be lost.

"Well, they left her monitor, dock station, keyboard, mouse... I think an officer took her laptop. I guess it's part of the investigation?" Dolfry shrugged and turned to get back to work. "Sorry."

An officer? The IT department should have taken it. There was no reason for the police to have it unless they thought Ava left something behind. Maybe a note in the disc drive, like with his? It was just more of a reason to get that laptop – fast.

There were two offices that they could be keeping it. One was in the basement, harder to get access to, while the other one was on the station floor in the main area. That one was easy enough with its corner location. He had gone in there once when he thought that his cell phone was lost, only to find it upstairs on the floor in his cubicle... under his desk.

Jack glanced down at his watch as he took the elevator back down to the main floor. He had tracked the officer's movements for weeks while he tried to find the man in the photo. That office should only have a clerk right now. With it being an open office with a counter across the front, anything extra would be easy to see on the desk in the back.

"Can I help you?" The woman looked up from behind the counter when the door opened. Jack hadn't exactly planned to interact with anyone. He was hoping just to walk in and out after getting a look. It took until now to realize how strange that would have been and surely someone would be after him. No need to draw more attention to himself.

Jack smiled politely. "I was wondering if a passenger came in about an hour ago. She asked me to help her find a charm bracelet. I told her to come here. I just wanted to know if she ever found it." It was getting impressive at how well he was lying now.

The woman flipped through the pages of the log book and Jack glanced at the desk against the back wall while she was distracted. There wasn't anything on the desk but a few papers and a monitor. The desk had a couple drawers. There was a chance it could be in there but there was no way Jack was going to be allowed back there to look.

"It doesn't look like anyone came in today." Jack needed to somehow get to those drawers. He could leap over the counter and knock the woman out with a karate chop to the back of the head, then get a look inside the drawers... and fly out with of the station with his newly inherited superpowers to match that heroic display of justice his mind just orchestrated.

"Maybe did someone turn in a bracelet? The woman seemed in a hurry but she said she was taking a train home later." He tried sending her mental messages of persuasion to get her to check the drawers in the desk. Knowing his luck, there was a box behind the counter for these sorts of things. "Maybe the officer put it in his desk to keep it safe. She did say it was a nice bracelet."

The woman checked the box, behind the counter like he feared. It was empty, but it wasn't like Jack expected her to find the imaginary jewelry there. Luckily, she got up and opened the drawers. There was no laptop in there either. The most striking thing he could see was an issue of Playboy, and a bright yellow stress ball in the shape of a duck.

He thanked the woman as he left. Things had gotten a whole lot harder. The basement office had one way in and one way out. Plus, to get to the basement, there was only one elevator that went that far down and an employee needed to swipe their ID card. If Dunn even suspected him, there was the nail in the coffin.

Jack grabbed an early lunch while he was away from his desk and tried to think things through. There was a slim chance that he'd be able to make it down without being seen, and even less of making it back out. That was one part that he couldn't monitor because that elevator ran the whole height of the building. The officers could get off anywhere and he had only focused on the mezzanine.

Chapter Twenty-Six

Jack had made it down to the basement on his way back. It was pure luck that someone else had used their ID to call down the elevator. While they had gotten off on the third floor, he had remained to ride it down to the basement instead. His card wouldn't show where he was. Not until he went to leave. The elevator was sure to be summoned by someone else before he could get back, but maybe Dunn would think an officer brought him down here. It really was the only plausible explanation.

It took him a moment to get his bearings. There were two paths from the elevator – down either direction of the hall. However, he could see one end and it stopped at what he could just make out on the door placard as 'Mechanical Room.' There were only a couple doors down that end of the hall but his gut told him the police office was the other way.

The hallway was eerily quiet given the fact that there were trains thunderously rolled by overhead on numerous tracks through the station. It only made him feel more uneasy about doing this. This wasn't who he was. He was just a guy who spent his days researching ways to prolong the useful life of rail, not covert spying.

Mentally, he cursed Ava. It was her fault for making him do this. If she hadn't died... if she'd just send the next clue *already*. Jack read the placard on the door he passed. So there was a mechanical room at one end and a bathroom with three more doors on this end. The next one he came to had a large, opaque glass window in the upper portion of the door with carefully painted words on the glass: *Amtrak Police Headquarters.*

He tried the door and found it to be unlocked. For as often as security was preached, the police seemed oddly lax in their own measures. Then again, only employees with an ID badge could summon the elevator and their movements were recorded somewhere. Jack knew he shouldn't be complaining about this momentary spurt of luck. If anything, there could be an officer waiting inside.

When the door opened, there was nothing but a couple desks with chairs and a few computers. Jack closed the door behind him and hit the little button in the doorknob to lock the door. It wasn't going to keep out any officers but it would buy him a little time, not that there was any place to hide in the office.

Jack walked to the closest desk but quickly realized that this wasn't Dunn's. There were poorly scribbled notes and a photo of an African American family smiling from the lone picture frame. He walked over to the other and froze. Open on the desk was a manila folder with Ava's employee photo clipped on one side and what was labeled the Medical Examiner's report on the other. It made him ill to think of how she died, that he let her down somehow. And underneath was a thin laptop, not connected to the dock station on the desk.

He set the file on the side and tried not to look at her smiling face. It was too much to deal with the emotions it was causing while he was breaking into a cop's office. Jack opened the lid and turned on the device. There should have been a screen asking for a password, but it just landed on her desktop. It was company policy to have a sign-in screen. It only meant that they were tampering with her laptop.

Jack tried to rush through the files, looking for anything Ava would have left for him. He knew that his time was short. He heard voices and he froze. If he got caught here, there were no plausible excuses. He could be fired, or worse… The voices headed into what he could guess was the bathroom and seemed to die down.

The search resumed. The urgency to rush was there but the risk that something was missed rose too. Jack was running out of ideas of where she'd have saved anything, if she had at all. Then his eyes saw a folder that was labeled *"Rail Lifespan Improvement."* That had to be it. Ava wasn't working on anything close to his work. He opened the folder and saw files. Files that looked to be largely images. Jack pulled out his USB flash drive and stuck it in the computer to copy the files. If they were what he could only hope they were, then Dunn could never see them. The file was sent to the trash bin after he stowed the flash drive and then purged.

He smiled and tried to set things how they were but the voices can back, and then someone tried the door. Jack closed the laptop cover and went to stand behind the door. It was no place to hide when whoever came in had closed the door. He'd still be in the open, but there was only under the desks to hide and it sounded like two voices. There was no place to hide when both spaces would be crowded with legs.

"Huh, John must have locked it." Jack could faintly make out someone saying. "He was making the rounds. It shouldn't be too long until he comes down. Let's just wait in the breakroom."

His ear was pressed against the back of the door as Jack strained to listen for their footsteps. He waited a couple moments, just to make sure. There wasn't much time with the threat of Dunn coming and knowing it was imminent. He unlocked the door and cautiously peeked out. The hallway was desolate. He made a break for the elevator and was just about the press the button when he heard the little beep that sounded at each level. It was coming down... and that meant Dunn.

Jack glanced around, looking for a place to hide, but there wasn't even a corner to dash around. There were only two places – the bathroom and the remaining mystery door. The chances of the mystery door worsening this situation was too great. He turned and slipped into the bathroom. The door barely closed when he heard the elevator open and someone getting off, talking on their phone. There was no mistaking that voice, and it felt like all the blood was draining from his body as it grew closer. Jack tried to remind himself that the office was just across the hall that Dunn had to come this far down.

His heart beat was pounding in his ears and time crept along. Jack squeezed the USB flash drive in his hand. He had to see what was on this and keep it safe. He had to get out of here. The office door opened and closed. Jack was going to make a move when he heard the other voices appear only to draw close and disappear. They had to be coming back for Dunn.

Jack took a couple deep breathes before leaving the safety of his bathroom hideout. He needed to get in that elevator. Once he made it to ground level, he'd be safe from questioning. He could do this. He had to. There was no turning back and sticking it out now.

The sensor on the elevator beeped that his ID was accepted. Jack kept glancing over his shoulder as the lift slowly crept down. Someone had to have heard that sound. There was no way he was going to be able to get away with this. The elevator chimed its arrival and he dashed inside, frantically hitting the button to close the doors. They finally clapped shut and the thing began to move up.

Jack couldn't wait to get back to the cubicle to check out the USB flash drive with the files he copied from Ava's computer. He had barely made it out of Dunn's office before he was caught. It was pure luck. Dunn's voice had been like nails on a chalkboard when the man spoke a few feet from the hiding place.

He turned the corner, seeing his space and knowing he was in the clear. As he walked into the cubicle, Jack almost had a heart attack. Five of his close coworkers were waiting to surprise him and, because of that, the flash drive almost went flying into the sea of temporary walls that separated them all from each other's space.

"Happy Birthday!"

With all the sneaking around today, he had been wound tight. It took a moment for Jack's heart to restart before he could laugh it off.

"You look like you forgot it was your birthday." His buddy slapped him on the back. "Now come get a slice of this cake before I eat it all." They all laughed, getting angered looks from the surrounding cubicles of uninvited drones.

This was nice though, for Jack. He felt normal and happy for a moment. There wasn't a worry as he took a piece of the cake with green frosting. It was just that he couldn't believe he forgot his own birthday. Jack glanced down at his watch to check the date, and his face fell a little as reality hit again.

"What's wrong, Jack? Don't like the frosting?" There were a couple chuckles still in the crowd as he shook his head.

"No, but why did you have to make it puke green?" Jack teased back. "Are you trying to say you miss seeing me like that?" They had been there thorough the rough times after Ava's death and fully knew how he looked, and about the lunches he tossed.

Chapter Twenty-Seven

Jack jumped a little when a box dropped onto his lap. "Happy Birthday."

He felt a kiss on his cheek as arms wrapped around him from over the back of the couch. It was his second birthday that they were celebrating together but he still hadn't expected a gift. For the first, she had surprised him with breakfast in bed.

"You know you didn't have to get me anything. Breakfast would have been good enough. I love your cooking." Jack patted the seat cushion next to him and a moment later Ava was next to him.

"You only say that because you can't cook." She laughed. There was a twinkle in her eye. "Go ahead. Open it already."

Jack laughed as he shook the box. "I can cook. I just chose not to." He paused as he tried to think of a good sounding excuse. "I chose not to... for the sake of my neighbors. I don't want them offended by any aromas, and I definitely don't want to share."

"You mean the smoke?" She teased and kissed his cheek. "Hurry up and open it. I want to know if you like it before I head home."

"Why are you leaving? I thought we were heading downtown to meet up with the guys from work for lunch." His fingers pulled off the ribbon. When Jack lifted the lid of the box, a face was staring back at him. He smiled as he took it out of the box.

"We are but I didn't think I'd ended up sleeping over last night; so, I don't have any clean clothes." Ava got up. Her feet still ached from dancing last night, but they weren't going to get any rest until tonight.

"I think you look fine." He smiled as he watched her pull on her shoes. Her dress swayed about her knees as she walked back over.

"You are just saying that so I won't leave." And the smile that grew on his face was proof that what she said was the truth. Ava tapped the face of his new watch. "Don't be late." She left him with one lingering kiss before she went out the door.

Chapter Twenty-Eight

Dunn sat in his chair and swiveled to face his computer monitor. Something felt off. He could have sworn that Koltrin's file wasn't left on that side of his desk. He could have asked his partner but Thorpe was too busy chatting with the officer that was relieving him. As much as he had fun with his partner, Dunn really wanted the man to leave. He needed time alone to focus as he dug through the girl's computer and finished the file. The IT department had finally got authorization to remove the password encryption.

He flipped open the lid and was confused. The laptop woke from its hibernation. Dunn knew that it wasn't left on. He hadn't been in his office for hours. It was his scheduled day to ride the on his territory. There was no way a laptop with half a battery could have lasted that long. Especially the laptops that were issued here.

"Thorpe, did you mess with this while I was gone?" If the computer was tampered with, maybe the file was too. He flipped through the pages, checking to make sure each numbered page was there and in order.

"Naw, I don't touch nothin' on your desk unless it's a donut. You can't leave those sittin' around. Vermin bait and all." The third cop laughed, but didn't confess to anything. Of course any officer had access here but something didn't sit right.

Inspector John Dunn entered into the employee access system. He knew something had happened today. Something since he made his rounds and security checks. The file wasn't in the neat stack on top of the laptop like when he dropped it off this morning; never mind that the laptop was running when he returned. If Thorpe hadn't touched it, not that he had any real reason to seeing as this wasn't his curse, then it had to be another employee.

It really wasn't a secret that there was an office in the basement, with the outlet office in the mezzanine for passengers. Only employees or someone who stole an ID badge could make it here. Either way there was a trail and he was going to find it. His partner thought he was being a bit paranoid. As if the air conditioning system had kicked in and booted up the laptop.

Dunn punched in his credentials and set the parameters for a search. He'd only search today's records before four o'clock and for this specific elevator. There was only one access point, so the results shouldn't be too massive. The only issue was that he couldn't filter by floor. That meant that someone could have come down from the fourth floor or ground level. Or they could have rode up from the basement level to any other one.

The list was rather extensive, even for just a few hours. He hated to think what daunting list would have resulted if it had been the whole day. The worst part was seeing how many repeat offenders used the elevators. One director from the Signal Department summoned the elevator ten times alone within those few hours.

He scrolled down, crossing off names on his mental list as he went. The mouse froze over one name though. Not even five minutes after Dunn came back to the office, fucking Jack Havest had called the elevator to the basement. That meant the man had been right here! Dunn could have nailed his ass.

Dunn stood up suddenly, his chair flipping over as the inspector stormed off. It was too late to pummel the whelp. If anything, he needed some fresh air and to calm his mind before making a call. He should have retired before all this shit hit the fan. The last thing he wanted to do was call a backstabbing politician, waking him or interrupting his evening cigar, after dealing with the annoying staff of Congressman Samuel Whitmore.

Chapter Twenty-Nine

He hadn't any time at work to look through Ava's files. The USB sat next to his computer. It was killing him not to have the next clue, and only his own collected information at his fingertips. There was one problem though. What if he didn't like what he found?

Could this file actually be about him? As far as Jack knew, there was nothing worth killing over what he was doing. It wasn't like rail lifespan and this new technology wasn't accessible to others doing the research; and others, in the company, were aware of his project. The catcher was that Jack knew about this secret, or at least what he thought was the secret, and yet there was no attempt at his life. He hated to think it, but maybe Ava had fabricated this all on her own and committed suicide. As much as it hurt, he'd almost rather that to be the truth. If not, she was dragging him willingly down the rabbit hole and he had no idea how far down it went.

Sitting there, staring as his computer screen wasn't going to make the decision for him or ease his mind in the least bit. Jack inserted the flash drive and saw the window pop up to ask him what he wanted to do. If only he knew.

There were over thirty folders, all labeled. There were photos and video, press releases and blogger's posts. Jack started with the photos, hoping they'd be the easiest. Already he could tell that some of this was already on the website that she left him. There were more photos of the sites, some taken during working hours and others at night via surveillance cameras. There were odd things in the latter with groups of huddled figures in the shadows.

Slowly, Jack was realizing how enormous of a mess Ava landed herself in. He didn't know how, but there really was no way out when the police were involved. Although, he couldn't make the connection between the Congressman and Amtrak, or the photos. An aging man like Dunn wouldn't be in shady parts during the middle of the night doing who knew what. It seemed like Ava knew but left the important pieces out of the files. How did she expect him to ever figure this out?

This mind was in complete overload. Jack could really use a drink right about now. Actually, that didn't sound like a bad idea to him. He could leave all of this back in his apartment and forget about it for a few hours. Jack got up to grab his jacket and wallet to head out to the pub.

Chapter Thirty

Jack had to drag her out. He had no idea why Ava suddenly wanted to stay in. Usually it was the other way around, but tonight was different. He had finally plucked up enough courage to ask her father for her hand in marriage. Not that he was going to tell Ava the occasion for celebration. No, she'd find that out soon enough.

Even once they got to the pub, it didn't seem like Ava's mood had lightened at all. The plan was to meet up with a few friends from work, enjoy a night out, get a little tipsy and refuse to let Ava leave alone that way. She was already going to be coming home with him when the night was over. She had her VCR there from movie night, and it was too bulky and awkward to haul along to the pub.

He saw their friends already at a booth and they meandered over. Ava slipped in next to her girl friend and he slid in next to her. They hadn't even been there a minute and she managed to have them all to laughing. Jack hadn't caught what Ava said. He was too lost in what happened earlier and what it meant for them. He leaned over and kissed her cheek.

"What's that for?" She laughed and leaned against him, a smile finally on her face.

Jack just shook his head softly. "Just because I can." God, how he loved her. The way she smiled. How she looked up at him with that spark in her eye. It was almost like he could see the love pouring out of those chocolaty orbs for him, or maybe it was the laughter lighting them up.

It looked like she was about to say something when the waitress came over to take their orders. They already had their go-to pub food order on standby: a plate of nachos, basket of fries, and four house burgers – medium-well done with caramelized onions, tomato, cheddar cheese and ranch dressing on a toasted sourdough bun.

"Getting the same tonight?" Jack asked her. Usually it was a Captain & Coke for her and a Samuel Adams Boston Lager for him, but Ava was shaking her head.

She leaned over closer to the waitress. "We'll have a Samuel Adams Lager and a Jack Rose."

Ava glanced at him out of the corner of her eye. He had no idea what she ordered, but the waitress must have known what it was. To him, it just sounded like a man's name. If he didn't know her better, Jack might have panicked and thought she was cheating on him. Although he was wondering where that drink, or even idea, came from.

Once the waitress left, he asked. "So is that the name of your secret lover?" Jack teased. It seemed to be the reaction that she hoped for as she moved back next to him. Ava shook her head and he pushed on, falling for the bait. It was hard not to when her mood was lightening back to what it normally was. "Then what is that Jack thing?"

"Jack Rose," she corrected. "One of the girls told me about it. It's a 'Jack' drink, so I had to try it." Ava smiled. "It has applejack, lime juice and grenadine. It's a brandy drink and tonight I feel like something a little sweeter."

There was something else under that statement. Maybe it had to do with earlier. Jack was almost sure that she wanted something sweeter to make the day better. He was definitely going to have to keep an eye on how much she drank tonight. There was no way that he was going to let her drown whatever it was in alcohol. He was right here, and he'd force it out of her somehow before letting it get that far.

The waitress returned with the drinks and nachos. He couldn't help but analyze this new drink along with the group. It looked like a nice cocktail with a cherry and apple slice garnish. Their friends were waiting for the verdict as Ava took a taste of the rosy colored liquid. He couldn't help but hoped it got the stamp of approval. After all, it had his name on it and he didn't want any negative connotation related to him. Not when he was after a life together with Ava.

"I think this might be my new favorite drink." Ava laughed a little. It was a relief to Jack. "Want to try it?" Her gaze landed on him.

Jack reached for the glass and took a sip. The sweet and tart hit his tongue, but it definitely was surprisingly good. "We might have to switch," he teased.

"Order your own." Ava grabbed her drink back and stuck out her tongue. He laughed and watched as she set it on her other side, far from him.

By the time the food arrived, the mood had improved at the booth and three more Jack Roses were annihilated by the table. For a few minutes, they were silent as they savored their burgers but then the conversation started up again. It seemed like there was a karaoke contest going, and it took eight songs for them to notice the placards on every table.

Jack grabbed one to read. "A hundred bucks. Ava, we have to do this!"

She just shook her head. Something still wasn't right with her. Ava sang all the time and now... he wasn't sure what else he could do to cheer her up. Was it him? She seemed happy once they got here with their friends, but she shied away when it was just going to be the two of them.

"Well, I'm doing it."

He got up and walked over to the booth to see what kind of selection they had. If Ava wanted to be a party-pooper tonight, he wasn't going to let it bring him down. Not when the day had put him on cloud nine. It was too great of a fall.

Jack flipped through the selection book as he looked for a song that he could sing to his future fiancé. When one particular song caught his eye. It was perfect. He was going to be her man, and save the day.

Ava glanced up. She recognized the song as Train's *Save the Day*. And much to her horror, it was Jack singing it. What was going through his mind lately? Then again she knew the only reason that question was floating around her mind was because of earlier. It wasn't just the karaoke; it was wondering why he was still with her.

Dunn had confronted her again; the threats mounting to staggering heights. Sure, Jack didn't know that she now had a very real and imminent expiration date, but it wasn't like she could really do much. Just give him a loving meal here and there and a VCR to watch their old favorite movies.

"I think she loves me," Jack crooned, "but it all depends."

His dance moves were horrendous. It was undeniable how much she loved him though. And the sight of him up on that stage, enjoying himself with a huge smile as she watched him, just put her in perfect bliss. She should be cherishing these moments more than what she was. Especially when he picked her favorite band; when Ava was sure that they'd have Queen or Smash Mouth or Barry Manilow, which happened to be his guilty pleasure.

Jack was really getting into it and Ava could see it was all for her. She smiled a little and tried to be positive encouragement for him. After all, he was putting on an otherwise ridiculous show.

Right now though, Pat Monahan's words were singing right to her soul. Jack wasn't going to be her Superman, but he was super in every other way. He couldn't save her, not when she couldn't save herself. Jack, or even

Superman, couldn't save her. All Ava could do was let the man she loved be with her and try to save him somehow. One day Jack might save someone else's day, but he could never save hers.

Monday morning, he was back to the grind. Not surprising that his boss wasn't sold singularly on the fact that the technology he was researching could extend the life of rail. There was another side to that coin, and the number of coins was what Jack had to figure out now. For every one question he answered, three more scenarios lurked.

He sighed as he stepped into the elevator. Sure it was faster to take the stairs, but he needed just a moment alone to enjoy the feeling of time slowly slipping by and nothing else. The few minutes were a luxury to waste.

Jack got off a couple floors down and headed down the hall to the Finance offices. Another daunting task of seeing too much information for his noggin, but this was for work and there was no way out of it. At least Jack had some idea of what to expect. There were going to countless invoices for steel prices that were going to have to be separated for its application; whether it was straight rail, switches, or frogs.

He showed his ID badge and explained what he needed to the woman behind the desk. She took him into the archives and directed him to the correct section in the webby catacomb of files. The sound of her quiet laughter as the door swung shut should have been an indication of how much he bit off. The rows of files towered over him, giving him the sense that he was being swallowed whole by its contents, by the room.

The best thing to do though was to dive right in. Jack had already decided that a ten year trend of rail prices should be enough for his second pitch to nab the technology. At least that eliminated half a row of the many. It was going to take hours of pulling files to sort them and record the numbers.

He couldn't help but look at the other documents in the files, noticing something else. There were quite a few large numbers. Now, a few hundred thousand wasn't really enough to be alarmed about. That was almost a common expense for any switch or rail project. It wasn't those prices that stood out, it was the opposite. There were enormous inflows of capital that far exceeded those large costs, enough to always put the company in the green financially.

It seemed that they started to appear around the time of the election. There were documented names of contributors when the amounts were in this large of quantities, but there was only one name that stuck out.

S. Whitmore.

Chapter Thirty-One

Dunn kept a close eye on the troublesome man. Not only had it been orders, but it was also out of spite. How had that clueless kid got pass him? Now it almost seemed like Havest knew what to stumble into. The girl's laptop was clean, so he had to have done something to it before Dunn could get at whatever was on there. So that could mean the girl talked after all. Only now the threat of killing Jack no longer worked, nor did the feuding lovers motive. Havest's death would need an entirely different cover story, meaning much more paperwork and headaches.

It had been weeks and the boy kept returning to the Finance archives. There hadn't been much to report other than that. Of course, Dunn had gone to the trouble of finding out what he was working on and it did fit the need to be poking around. Although, there was a paranoid little voice in the back of his head telling him there was no coincidence when it came to Havest anymore. The male had outsmarted his once, with his office espionage, and Dunn wasn't going to allow a repeat of that.

As suspicious as it might have been, he was personally going into the archives on his own time at night to see what files Havest had pulled that day. He wanted to know exactly what information was at the boy's hands. Unfortunately, he was pulling enough files to cause a problem. If the boy looked at anything more than the rail invoices, he might make a connection, and depending on what Koltrin let slip, Havest might figure everything out.

He was definitely going to have to handle Havest. It was just a matter of how. If word got up the chain of power, then there was no option that wasn't akin to the girl's fate. Maybe he could scare the boy, unlike the girl, he might be smart enough to stop digging around.

Chapter Thirty-Two

Jack held his head in his hands as he sat, once again, at his computer desk. It always ended the same. He'd come here, sit with his head cradled in his hands, fight with himself to look at Ava's files, give up and grab a beer. It seemed that lately it could be called a problem.

Only this time he knew that he needed to stop playing this standstill game. He sat down with his beer and open up the folder on his desktop that he created for this whole crazy mess. He was able to skip the video. Ava already gave him all that on VHS tape. Most of the photos were nondescript, unimportant or used in the hefty document she already dropped into his lap. At least this time around though, he was able to make more of the connections to the Congressman versus before when Jack thought the biggest thing she was telling him was that she was getting into politics.

It all seemed to fall into place though, but Jack couldn't help feeling that there was more missing. This was just hearsay. Even with the blogs, it seemed that it only added more to the feeling of being a conspiracy theory. Yet, Jack knew there were real possibilities behind it all. He had seen the figures in the archives. The problem now was providing it on the other side. Maybe that's what Ava finally unturned. That would be enough to kill for, especially with what was at risk for the Congressman and the company. If that wasn't on her work computer, she had to have stored it somewhere else.

It took Jack a moment, but then he realized what Ava would have done. If he was meant to find it, then it would be on her personal computer. There was no way that the Amtrak police could get their hands on that. Especially not after this was considered a suicide and wrapped up tight, as far as anyone was concerned. The only problem was that Ava no longer had an apartment. He could only hope that her family didn't discard it when they went through her things. Then again, maybe it was already wiped clean and whatever it was that she wanted him to know was forever gone.

He grabbed his cell phone. This was going to be painful. Not only had they lost Ava, but they had lost all connection to him too. To top it off, Jack had stolen so much of her time and life. There was no choice anymore though. There seemed to never have been a choice.

"Hello?" Her father picked up on the third ring, and his heart fell into the bubbling acid of his stomach. "Hello? Anyone there?"

Jack took a deep breath. "It's Jack."

There was a long pause, as if the man was running through every Jack he knew. Maybe he was. It wasn't like they call each other much before or after her death but it seemed to dawn on him who was on the phone.

"Jack." He could almost imagine the painful smile on the aging man's face. This wasn't easy on him when Ava was such a daddy's girl. "How are you doing?" Even though it was just small talk, it was just as painful.

"I'm surviving." That was all that it could be called. Other than Ava's breadcrumb trail, he didn't get out and live much outside of work. He was back to the desolate group of two friends that he had before her, and who bore no real burden of ever conversing, outside of an event happening in town every month or so. "I need a favor." He paused. It sounded like a horrible thing to say, but the shorter this painful call was the better for the both of them to do what they needed to forget again.

"Did you take Ava's laptop?"

After a pause, came a disheartening reply. "No, Jack. I didn't see it."

Jack sighed. Maybe somehow the police had gotten it. That meant that it was all over. He should have been relieved but it was more depressing. He had let Ava down and had no explanation for why she was taken from him. She was supposed to be engaged to him now and planning their wedding, damn it! She wasn't supposed to be alone and cold in the unloving ground.

"Jack, her brother might have taken it. Let me give him a call. If he took it, I'll have him get it to you. Was there anything in particular you were looking for?"

It was hard not to appreciate the man's consideration and offering of hope, but Jack couldn't take it. He knew that this was the end. All he was going to be able to do now was visit her grave and lay his flowers on her headstone. How long could he make the pilgrimage to where she lay? And when he was a graying man at the end of his existence, would he be able to lay next to her forever?

He tore open the envelope and smiled when he saw the lone disc. Ava's brother was awesome. Then again, so was her whole family. They practically took him in as one of their own while they dated, and it seemed like even more so now. It didn't even take two days for her brother to copy the files and get it in Jack's hands, being halfway across the country.

Although maybe it was more to make up for all the heckling he gave Jack over the years. Her brother was a tad bit overprotective of the auburn firecracker. He had wanted to make sure his little sister had the best and that Jack gave her it all. But nothing seemed to have been enough to gain the brother's true acceptance until he made his intentions quite clear to her family.

Now it was all just one more thing to hide in the recess of his mind with the rest of it. All that he'd remember now was that he owed her family one. Maybe figuring this all out would be enough. It would give him peace, and surely they could take some from it as well.

Jack popped the disc into his laptop, hoping that there was something there to help him.

Chapter Thirty-Three

The door was barely closed when their lips met again. Ava didn't have a problem with the furry ape pressing up against her. The fur from his King Kong costume tickled her skin again as he moved. Her laugh just made a smile appear on his lips.

"Are you laughing at King Kong?" He whispered between hurried kisses. Jack's arms wrapped around her waist. His fingers ran over her soft skin above the seam of her jeans and just under the faux torn shirt that Kong was supposed to have ravished.

"What if I am?" She challenged, but Jack pinned her up against the door they barely made it through. Maybe it was the alcohol from the Halloween party they left that made him bolder tonight. Or maybe it was something entirely different that changed within Jack. But tonight, there was a primal, dominating spirit that had taken over the ape man.

"I'm going to have to bring out my tower." It was a low growl that echoed in Ava's mouth as he barely broke a kiss to utter his threat. But words didn't need to be said for her to know what King Kong was going to do with the damsel he stole. She could feel the growing difference through the cheap costume rental.

It was a surprise when Jack moved his lips from hers and found the delicate skin of her neck. Her face blushed when she realized the soft noises were escaping her throat. Any rational, sane thoughts between them were over. Her hands scoured his back for the zipper to the costume.

It felt like such a major victory when her fingers finally located it and started the descent. A chill ran down her spine when she felt the hot breath on her neck as a laugh played against her skin. "I don't think so." Jack lifted her and smirked when her legs automatically wrapped around his waist.

He carried her deeper inside the apartment and gently placed her on the bed. He couldn't tell if it was the spark between them or the hairy costume making him hot. But this time Jack let her wandering fingers drag the zipper down. All that he had under the costume were his briefs. It just gave him more time to focus on removing Ava's shreds she called clothing. He couldn't believe they lasted through the party, much less having agreed to let her out like that. His fingers trailed down her side as he claimed her mouth again. The slight touches seemed to only make Ava greedier in her need for him.

Jack moved away from her to stand and let the costume fall from him. He watched as she sat propped up on her elbows, her eyes hungry for him. There was not a sliver of doubt in his mind that Ava wanted him completely. He watched her eyes travel down over his body, taking in his average physique before stopping at his loins where a battle was being fought to restrain him.

He reached down to remove the last bit of white clothing, letting it join the bunch of fur on the floor. A smirk worked onto his face as he watched Ava's eyes grow wide, but she wasn't running. It slowly sank in that maybe reality struck Ava and she didn't want this with him anymore.

Then she scooted to the edge of the bed. Her eyes were still glued to the part of his body standing at attention and his was on the beauty wearing only black underwear. To his surprise, Ava reached out and touched him. He had to close his eyes and think of hairy old ball sacks just so he didn't lose it right them. He could feel her fingers gently running along his length and back to the tip.

"Ava," he spoke in a strained whisper. This wasn't how it was supposed to be. He was supposed to be slipping into her by now, proving to her with each thrust that she was his. She wasn't supposed to undoing him so easily and reducing him to putty in her hands with just a simple touch. He didn't know if it was just the desire or having waited so long to be with her that was wrecking this havoc.

Jack felt something moist and warm. His eyes flew open. Gazing down in shock and awe, he watched as his tip disappear into her mouth. Then a little more vanished before she moved back and let him slip out of that newfound paradise.

She was just shaking her head, her nose scrunched up, and he knew tonight was over. "You taste like bologna."

They stared at each other for a moment as it set in. It was so ridiculous and they couldn't stop the sudden, crippling laughter from taking over. Ava fell back on the bed, holding her stomach, while Jack was bent over and barely able to stand.

It took him a moment less to get back under control and he knelt over her on the bed, watching the last of her giggles escape. "I'm never going to be able to eat bologna again," he chuckled and kissed her softly.

When he broke the kiss, Ava leaned up to seal her lips over his, begging him to come closer. His hand ran slowly down along her side. Jack stopped for a moment at her hip when he grazed the dark cotton. He had to part from her soft lips and her eyes opened slightly, as if to protest in their own little way. It was unavoidable. The panties had to be sent packing with the rest of their clothing. Jack slid them off and watched as she hurried it along by removing her devious bra, tossing it over the edge of the bed.

He gazed down at her pale, rosy skin. She was perfect. Perfect for him. It was like a dream when she blushed, seeing him drinking her in with his eyes. "Jack..." She was embarrassed, and so cute with the downward turned gaze. He crept back up her body and kissed away her embarrassment. There was no room for that here.

As he moved between her legs, Ava placed a hand on his chest. It felt like something was weighing on her other than his lips, getting more passionate by the second. Jack could feel her soft skin of her inner thigh brush against his erection as his body urged him onward.

He rolled his hips, brushing against her in a way to pull a slight groan from his mouth and a shiver from her body.

The hand on his chest shifted and traveled down his chest, running the length of his side. Her fingers exploring and finding their place on his back as he reached down between. Jack almost jumped at his own touch. He was wound so tight, between the alcohol and Ava. He was positioning himself when her other hand pressed to his chest. That must have been what caused her to hesitate. Maybe she doubted what they had. Maybe the alcohol made her forget. But it was so easy to remind her before he took his sweet time showing her and making sure that she never forgot again.

"I love you, Ava." It was a whispered on her lips as he barely slipped in with a roll of his hips.

Ava gasped and her eyes found his, slightly alarmed for a moment by the new sensation. But she didn't stop him. Nothing could stop them. It was just the realization sobering them up for a moment, reminding him of their promise and of what was to come. The promise they'd be gentle with each other on their first time; the future where she became his.

Jack gently traced his fingers over her gentle features in the soft morning's glow that crept in through the window. The soft touch of her lips under his thumb. How her brows gently furrowed on her otherwise peaceful face while she slept. He tucked a stray piece of hair behind her ear.

Ava shifted a little and for a moment, he feared that he woke her. She wouldn't like that he was watching her sleep. But she didn't wake. Ava only snuggled closer to him. There was just something about the subconscious gesture of wanting to come closer into his warmth and the safety of his arms. Something that warmed his heart, as to say her love would only be for him.

He couldn't help the smile that grew on his face. Jack was completely and utterly in love with the auburn beauty. And it just wasn't the alcohol buzz making him think that. In a month, he was going to drop to his knee and ask her to be his forever. And laying here with her, he knew that he couldn't wait to spend every moment of his life with her.

Chapter Thirty-Four

Jack couldn't believe it. He stared at it all. Everything that he hunted for over a month was going to be delivered in two days. Worst part was that she even made a note why the wait: *to give Jack a chance to back out and find something to make him happy.*

"Damn it, Ava. If you put as much effort in living as you did this," he groaned. This whole thing was so thought out. Clearly, there was a way that she could have stayed alive, even with the police hunting her. Jack knew what she had and yet he was still flying under the radar.

He tried to push the feeling that she abandoned him by scrolling through a public record of financial reports that Ava had filed. Even a simple report seemed to have stolen so much of her efforts and it angered him. She had apparently asked an accountant friend from college to go through and annotate it to make sense of the data.

Jack got up to toss a frozen dinner into the microwave. The box eating his counter space hummed to life as he paced. He couldn't believe that he was actually starting to hate the woman he was so whole-heartedly in love with. The survivor's guilt he originally felt was so consumed by anger of abandonment he was now feeling. He wished for himself to stop and let her death be for nothing.

The microwave beeped and he begrudgingly yanked the pasta dish out, grabbing a fork on his way back to the computer. Jack plopped down in the chair and tried to find some kind of file that he hoped wouldn't hurt him as much as the last one had, but it seemed that his luck wasn't going to allow it.

What opened up was something that truly rattled him. Probably more than finding out what kind of goose he'd been chasing the whole time. It was Ava's whole damn schedule for her damn clues! Jack reached for his cell phone. He didn't want to believe it. Was there anyone that wasn't in this elaborate scheme?

He dialed the number he called countless times. And even after her death, that number didn't get any reprieve. It probably got more action as he sought to hear her voice one last time.

Like always, it rang. And rang. And rang.

"Hello?"

Jack froze. It was a male voice. A boy. It sounded so familiar, but he couldn't put his finger on it. Ava definitely didn't have any kids, and neither did her brother. There was no way to explain the person on the other end, male or female, when this was his dead girlfriend's number.

"Hello?" Jack could hear another voice in the background. He strained to hear even more. Someone had Ava's cell phone. Someone who hadn't picked up at all these past months. Someone who might have known something, anything, to ease his mind.

"Mikey, I told you not to play in here and... Are you on that phone?" It was a woman's voice, definitely older. But it was her words.

Jack hung up. He knew exactly where her cell was. What he couldn't figure out was why. He had just met the boy when he slipped on the icy sidewalk. The boy hadn't known who he was then, so how would either of them have known Ava? Every time she had crossed the town's border; he had stolen her completely from the rest of the world.

Should he pound on their door and demand answers? Would they have anything to offer him after hiding for so long? Jack sighed and ate his pitiful dinner. He'd talk to them tonight, after he had time to cool down and process.

He waited impatiently at the door. Jack knew they were home. Hell, it hadn't even been ten minutes since he called Ava's cell. He was too impatient with this whole thing to bother to think and he was still fuming in the hallway.

The sound of a deadbolt sliding away and the click of a lock was the only indication that this might be over. Slowly, incredibly slow, the door open. A sandy blonde haired woman opened the door. Her face flushed with recognition, and something else. Guilt? Maybe that was hopeful thinking and imagination on his part.

"I'm Jack Havest. 3B. I think you know why I'm here." He said firmly. The levelness of his voice surprised him. What he felt like doing was shoving this woman up against a wall until he knew everything. Something about the way she meekly stood in the doorway made him reconsider that option.

"Hi, Jack." The little boy came to stand next to his mother. That little face smiled up at him, only this time Jack couldn't offer anything back.

"I guess we haven't officially met. My name is Cora Sanderson, and this is my son Michael." She let her arms gently hug the little boy. "Ava told us a lot about you."

His hands balled up at his sides. How could she talk so casually right now? This wasn't a friendly house call to swap recipes or invite them over to play charades; although, this was feeling like the biggest charade of all time.

"Don't talk about her," he grumbled out. "I want her cell phone back. It's not yours."

"And it's not yours." The woman retorted. "Ava needed help and I offered to-"

"You're damn right she needed help!" Jack snapped. He forgot about the boy until he saw the woman cover her son's ears and glare disapprovingly.

"I can understand why you're angry, but you will not use foul language in front of my son. You can come in and we can talk but when I ask you to leave, you leave."

It seemed with great reluctance that Cora move aside. Even little Mikey seemed to have a different opinion of him now and left to his room. Or what Jack guessed his room from the sound of a door closing deep in the apartment. He went over to the couch and sat to wait for Cora to join. There was a million and one questions he wanted to ask. A million and one things he wanted to yell at her for. She had pushed him just as far as Ava had without even knowing him.

Cora came and sat in a chair kitty-corner to him. She probably felt safer with more space between them. Jack knew he made himself out to be an idiotic tyrant in their first real meeting.

"I'm sorry about earlier." Jack sighed. "It's just... this whole thing is getting to me. She put together this whole stupid thing instead of trying to stay with me and then I find out that three doors down is where all the answers are."

The woman didn't seem fazed by his apology, but he could see she was itching to say something. She was probably to reprimand him for the hasty visit and vulgar outburst. "I still want her cell phone back."

Cora shook her head. "She gave it to me. I need it." She could see the anger boiling inside the man and quickly explained. "I lost my job a while back and had asked Ava to borrow hers. I remembering saying that I wish I still had one to stay in contact with Mikey's school and to help with the job hunting. Ava used to let me borrow it during the week while she used her company phone and spent time with you. I wasn't allowed to answer her calls or listen to the messages, and I'd give it back when she came to visit you. One day she said I could just keep it if I did her a favor. I had no idea what was going to happen... or what she planned to have me do to you." The woman sighed and looked to her fidgeting hands in her lap. "She gave me a timeline and scripted texts to send. It's on the counter if you don't believe me."

He did though. He knew exactly what that timeline looked like because he saw the original document on the disk from her personal laptop. "I'm supposed to be getting a packet of financial reports. Why don't you just give them to me and whatever those last few things on the list are?"

Jack sighed and looked to the woman. She seemed a little confused.

"The only things I have left are the reports and I mailed them this morning. Maybe someone else is doing those?" Of course, there was one more thing she was holding onto. The girl had made her promise, out of everything, that this last letter would be delivered once it was over; whether Jack wanted to find the truth or not. It was one that might never be delivered and couldn't be read a moment before.

"You should be getting them in the next couple of days."

He was at his wits' end. If it didn't feel like he was so close to the end, then Jack would have just given up. For good this time. This whole orchestrated mess was just making him hate the one person he let into his life and loved.

Silently, Jack stood and headed for the door.

As Cora watched the man walk away glumly, she couldn't help but think of the girl. That day had been so embarrassing for her and Ava was practically a saint. If she hadn't already been envious of the girl for having it all together, that day made it worse. The girl had a decent man in her life and not a child from getting knocked up senior year. Not that Cora would give up her son for the world or a second chance.

When a single mother loses her job after getting to work twenty minutes late because her son forgot his bag lunch and she had to stop, out of the way, at the school, there was no way to avoid being envious. Or when she started bawling like a baby with the little bit of sympathy the girl had given her.

Girl! She had to stop thinking of Ava as such. In truth, they could only be a few years difference between them. The only thing making her feel old were the years of countless sleepless nights and stress of raising a proper, decent boy instead of the asshole that got her drunk at a club and ditched her ass on the side of a road after they woke up in the back seat of his car.

Cora had bawled that day, and she was bawling when she officially met Ava. It was just as the battery on her cell phone went dead as she was talking to the babysitter. She had gone to the vestibule of the commuter train to take the call and avoid the eavesdroppers. That's why she cursed so loudly, and caused Ava to jump as she moved between cars, thinking a stranger was a crazy psycho going to spaz out on her.

Of course once Ava said those three words – *Are you alright?* – Cora let out her whole life story. It was just so easy to let it out with her. She poured out how Mikey was being bullied in school, getting detention and that she had to make sure the nurse made him take his asthma medicine. Then came out the financial troubles with keeping up with the doctor bills, paying rent, and how she was screwed now that she lost her job at a popular cheese steak joint.

And somehow this "perfect life" girl embraced her, physically and emotionally, and let her cry it all out until the train arrived at her stop. Of course it was their stop. Ava was no doubt on her way to see Jack. She had seen it almost daily. The way she'd trek out here to see him before going out together to someplace probably wonderful. The pair was inseparable, and now she was wasting time on a pathetic human being instead of Mr. Wonderful.

It had been then that Ava offered to help; actually, to do more than that. She volunteered to babysit Mikey. She was going to loan out her personal phone, with a set of rules of course. Ava was even going to pay her. And for what in return? Just a simple favor, as Ava put it. Just to mail a few packages and deliver a special letter. Cora had joke that she'd do anything that kept her clothes on if it would get her through it all and give her son the best life she could.

The next day, Ava had stopped over after dinner with Jack, leftovers in hand that were still hot, which Mikey devoured. It was then that she went over the plan, the secrecy needed. Her eyes were so laden with sadness that Cora felt her heart breaking. What could have caused this angel so much pain?

Until that day, Cora hadn't seen such pain in anyone be-sides herself. She and Mikey were getting back on their feet. Things were finally turning around and life going back to normal. They were happy again. But the same couldn't be said for the man who just left. His eyes were just like Ava's. Sad. Lonely. Lost.

Chapter Thirty-Five

Jack opened his mailbox on his way up to the apartment after an unimpressive day at work. There was a large manila envelope taking up the whole space. He pulled it out and noticed the postal stamp. *Narberth*. It was only because he was expecting the reports his neighbor promised would arrive that he bothered to notice. Exactly two days later, it had arrived. For going three doors down a hallway, the postal service was lagging.

For curiosity's sake or rather to prove it was what he thought, Jack ripped open the top and glanced inside as he took the stairs up towards his place. He flipped through the first couple pages and confirmed it was the financial reports from Ava's computer. He sighed as he unlocked the door and walked inside. Jack tossed the whole thing in the recycling bin.

They were pointless now that he already figured it out. If this was Ava's last hint, what was he supposed to figure out? He had learned from the records that the Congressman was secretly funding the company. How was that worth dying over, even if it was just gracious donations? It wasn't just that though. It was embezzlement from campaign funds, from the state. But so what? There were government watchdog groups for that kind of stuff.

"Whitmore stole money to buy us a train, Ava. They wouldn't kill over that. Who did you piss off?" It had to be that. She annoyed the wrong person and maybe threatened their paycheck. In this economy, it was probably enough to justify murder and Ava was troublesome when an idea got in her head.

Jack sighed and went to grab the leftover Chinese food from the fridge to pop into the microwave. At least now, with Ava gone, he wouldn't have to listen to her nag over his poor nutritional choices. So what if he like extra soy sauce to smother his rice with? It was full of sodium and that was a preservative, so it would just make him live forever. Ava was more likely to give him a heart attack, especially with all this stuff she stirred up since her death.

The microwave wailed when the timer went off. That was the only thing on his mind lately. He only thought of the food and how much he hated Ava these days. He had been distracted by those thoughts as he walked over, bumping into the recycling bin. The packet of reports that just arrived from his neighbor spilled out. Jack cursed as he picked up the papers. A name happened to catch his eye as he shoved the reports back into the bin.

John Arthur Dunn.

Chapter Thirty-Six

He kicked up his feet on the desk. This new job was cushy. Definitely a smart move for a cop in his thirties and with a new wife at home, giving him grief over a city job with demanding hours. At least here, Dunn had almost the same wages, plus additional benefits and a steady work schedule. That made the attempts to conceive easier to fit the optimum ovulation schedule from the obstetrician.

Dunn's radio crackled to life. *"Officer Dunn, we got a call from a homeowner claiming someone is lying motionless in the tracks around milepost eight dot nine in North Philly. Can you respond?"*

A man twenty years younger, and unaware of the mess he was just joining, accepted the call and got ready to head out of the office.

North Philadelphia didn't always have the best areas, and it was that which gave it such a bad reputation. "Brotherly love" definitely wasn't the unwritten rule in these parts. Word of gang activity and illegal dog fighting were almost synonymous with North Philly these days.

Fortunately, it was during the day and, generally, a time when the area was less dangerous.

Dunn parked the cruiser. There was ton of trash from people dumping on the railroad's property. Not that he was so delusional to think everywhere was pristine. He was expecting this to be a wild goose chase, or maybe just a doll of some sort that had fooled the homeowner. But as he drew closer, the stench was more apparent. There was something dead in the area. It could be an unlucky pigeon that fried itself on the overhead catenary wires. That might be too much of wishful thinking at this point, given what he saw surrounding him. Then the unsettling macabre sight of a twisted, contorted human arm came into view rising between the rails of the track, like it was waving.

The young officer felt ill instantaneously as he reached out for a catenary pole to stead himself. His voice felt foreign as he stuttered and stammered while he called in the report, asking that trains in the area to be stopped. It was the first time that Dunn had seen something so heinous. The worse during the city job was the sewer patrols and homeless. This just left him at a complete loss. This wasn't anything close to any kind of training that he ever received.

The train dispatcher came back over the radio to inform him that a crew to clean up the scene was on their way and all trains were halted.

"What do I do now?"

John Dunn finally made it home. He had spent the last three hours after work in the bar downing a bottle of whiskey. It had been a flood of rumors on the nightly news, all saying that the body was a mob hit. Not that it was a surprising rumor for that area. By tomorrow morning, it was probably going to be discovered to be a suicide. Not that it made the image any easier to swallow or forget.

He unlocked the door to the small suburban house and went inside. It was pitch black and he knew his wife had gone to her friend's to spend the night. She must have expected him to return home drunk and didn't want any part of that. So much for the scheduled sex tonight that was going to take his mind off of work. Not that he could blame her for leaving. Dunn wasn't a pretty sight when he was drunk, but somehow his wife had overlooked that long enough to marry him.

Dunn stumbled into his armchair only to jump up. He turned as a light blinded him. The light in the living room was suddenly flipped on and, when his eyes readjusted, he saw three large, burly men in his room. One occupied his armchair that a moment ago he tried to sit in, and that was the one to speak to him.

"John Arthur Dunn, thirty-six, newlywed and already in debt." It was a slap in the face, and meant to be a wake up all. These men knew who he was. Dunn wouldn't be surprised if they knew what he ate for lunch. The little show of information was enough to seal his suspicions; and, they were the same as the second rate reporter. This was mob related.

"Now you're in a rough spot, Johnny." The man in his armchair cracked his knuckles. One of the other men pushed him down onto the couch. Fear was quickly sobering him up.

"Wh-what are you d-doing in my h-home?" John stammered out.

The man in his chair, the one he assumed to be the leader, laughed. "That's up to you Johnny. Either you'll sign our contract or my associate here will but a bullet between your eyes. Think about that pretty little wife of yours and what she'll think when she comes home and finds you like that."

The man managed to wear a grim smirk the entire time he spoke and Dunn didn't doubt his words for a moment. While he had no idea what this contract might be, he knew that there was no choice. These people had to know he was a cop, and yet still came here. Not that he trusted himself to unload his magazine into any of these men, if he managed to get his handgun out of his holster in his condition.

Dunn hiccupped, out of fear and intoxication. "I'll sign it."

He knew better than to ask to read it. Even if he knew exactly what was in it, there was no option B. At least he could sign it now, get them out of his house, and then he'd fix this in the morning. Get some back up from his old force or something.

The large man on the left pulled a rolled document from his breast pocket and a pen. The thug smoothed the paper out on the coffee table and held the pen out to Dunn.

Chapter Thirty-Seven

Jack stared at the reports. He understood why Dunn was involved now. The reports started in the seventies and were yearly after that. They showed when he switched jobs and came to Amtrak. It wasn't hard to see how rough the economy was rough, and he could only imagine what a newlywed went through. For a moment, Jack wondered what it would have been like for himself. It probably wouldn't have been much of a change, financially, at all.

She gave him the last piece, the last bit that seemed to clear things up. This was all because of Dunn. Something started decades ago with the cop and it built up to something that got her killed. Somehow it felt like this was going to be easier. All he had to do was rifle through Dunn's life with a fine tooth comb, returning the favor.

The only problem was that this was more or less illegal. Thus far, Ava had been merely passing along intel. An online search would only yield so much, and nothing that would put together the last pieces. Jack doubted the old man even would make a blip on the internet. Dunn probably didn't know how to even boot up a computer.

He got up from the couch and slipped them into his work satchel. Jack wanted to read them again when he wasn't emotional or exhausted. Glancing at the clock, it was nearing eleven. Sighing, Jack resigned for the day.

In the morning, what Jack took could barely be considered a shower. From the moment he was stripped of clothing to when he was buttoning the last one on his shirt couldn't have been more than two minutes. For once, in a long time, Jack was looking forward to work. Not because it had somehow become more fulfilling or a huge leap had been made overnight. He knew there was a stack of papers that were going to give him his life back. One that would be almost as good as when Ava still existed.

He grabbed his work bag and locked up. On the way out of the building, Jack glanced at his neighbor's door. To think that the good mood he was in now almost didn't happen if the Sandersons skipped out on one of Ava's requests. It made him wonder for a moment what would have happened if Ava never met them or if Cora Sanderson was so upset over his spontaneous visit to raid his mailbox to get these reports.

The commute to the office wasn't too bad. Jack even followed the old routine and took the route pass Ava's old cubicle. The sting was long gone and, if anything, it felt good. If only she was sitting in front of that computer so he could tell her how awesome she was. How amazed he was at the whole thing she put together. How he was going to pay her back for this whole thing. It would all just have to wait until they met on the other side.

Jack set his bag on the desk next to his computer and pulled out the envelope with the reports. He knew there were a few deliverables due this week for his project, but he couldn't help his curiosity. He booted up his computer and pulled up the file with the notes he had found. Scrolling through what he already deciphered, there were pages and pages of financial reports. Things that had to do with the company and with Dunn's personal finances. Although, he really couldn't make much sense out of it. How was this really going to help him?

He groaned and leaned back in his chair. Somehow Ava had figured this out, or knew someone who could. That left him with nothing to do, except his actual work. Jack was sure, for most of his career, it had been exciting work. Since losing Ava, he couldn't care less about it. At the same time, he knew his boss was counting on this work getting completed, so he trudged on.

"Jack, you heading down for lunch?"

He glanced up to see his buddy standing in the doorway of his cubicle. Their friendly group lunches were something that he had been trying to get back into. At first, it had been torture without Ava and they all always had on faces of concern over how he was handling it.

"Sure, just let me..." He started to minimize the open documents, as he locked the computer screen, Jack saw the reports. "Hey, Connor, you any good at figuring out old financial reports?"

Chapter Thirty-Eight

He looked so smug sitting there eating his cheesesteak. He had waited until his friends headed back to work. He walked up to the round table and dropped the manila folder in front of him.

"Open it," he ordered.

Jack was startled and it shown in his shaky hands as he abandoned the last mouthful to open the folder. He started to gag at what was inside and tossed the folder back.

"What the hell?" He shouted.

Dunn sat down and slid the folder back across the table. "It's Koltrin's autopsy report." He flipped open the cover and turned over the color photos of the girl pinned against the platform and the gory mess after they got her out. That wasn't what this meeting was about.

"I know we've had our differences and I'm sticking my neck out for you." Dunn was getting too old for this shit. "This is your last chance to just walk away and get rid of all you have." Dunn flipped through the report to page eleven and pointed out a section. "Think about what you lost. It's not worth playing this game."

He got up, leaving Jack to debate reading the report or trashing it. Obviously Dunn was using whatever it contained as a ploy to get to him. It had to be a trap. That's the only thing this folder was but Jack couldn't curb his curiosity. The report in front of him looked legit, but anyone with a computer could have printed something out on letterhead paper; and yet, he had to know.

Jack started instead from the beginning of the section Dunn pointed out. The report seemed harmless enough. It was things he already knew, such as Ava fell into the track area from the platform and that cause of death was extreme blunt force trauma. Part of him was a little disappointed that there was no gunshot wound or substances in her system to make sense of why she jumped. It was just hard to imagine Ava purposefully jumping in from of a train, even knowing Dunn had something to do with the whole thing. Although, Jack doubted that was really what he was supposed to take away from this ploy – that Dunn was innocent in her death.

There was a short list of things Ava had in her possession, but nothing unusual. Except that if she was catching the train to go north, that she didn't have her purse with her. But at the end of the medical examiner's list, where Dunn had pointed, was a word that punched him in the gut.

Note: While body showed no signs and autopsy was inconclusive, blood tests show hormone levels consistent with pregnancy. Estimated one month.

Jack couldn't take his mind off those words. He was going to be a father. There was supposed to be a little baby in his arms right now. There was supposed to be little giggles and tiny clothing all over the apartment. There was supposed to be a wonderful auburn-haired girl by his side, smiling.

Chapter Thirty-Nine

Ugh... not today.

Ava hit the snooze on her alarm. She wanted another few hours of sleep, even though that was going to be impossible. She had to be at the office in an hour.

Her stomach lurched for the third morning in a row and Ava ran down the hall to the bathroom. She barely made it to the toilet when the heaving started. It always only lasted a few minutes and left a horrible taste in her mouth, even after she brushed her teeth.

Something just didn't feel right. Sure, yesterday was understandable. Ava had a huge presentation later that morning and her partner had been out sick the whole week. There had been extra pressure all week, but today? Today was just strange. Her alarm started rioting down the hall and she grumbled on her way back to silence it for good.

Her morning ritual was hurried through by shortcuts that she debated redoing at work, like her hair. With Jack gone this week to Harrisburg for some rail thing, she hadn't put in the extra bits of effort. Just a bit of eyeliner and blush to make her look awake, and a nice floral print dress to soften her chignon hairstyle. It was just a fleeting thought on her way into work. Was she pregnant?

She couldn't be! You'd have to have sex to get pregnant and... There was that one time on Halloween with Jack. He was her first, so there wasn't much to think about who it could have been. That night was a bit hazy from the alcohol, but she knew it happened and they had to have used a condom. Jack always carried one since he met her father. She had managed to break one of them down enough to get the story, and it was either take the condom or face death if anything ever happened.

It seemed like she couldn't focus on anything but the possibility. Her feelings about it flip-flopped so much, and all the blinking cursor on the computer monitor did was taunt her. She had already texted Jack to wish him a great day and ask how he was doing. She decided against telling him she felt sick again this morning. There was no need to get him worried about nothing. But by lunch, Ava couldn't take it anymore. She skipped out on lunch with their friends and headed a few blocks down the street to the convenience store. All she had to do was get a pregnancy test and prove that this was all in her head. She headed down the aisle, to the back, and froze when she saw the pregnancy tests, and condoms, under lock and key behind a glass wall.

"I help you?" An elderly Chinese woman walked up next to her.

"Yes. I, um... I need a pregnancy test."

It was clear to see the judgment in the old woman's eyes, and Ava was willing to bet the Chinese she mumbled was about her. She watched as granny unlocked the door and slide the glass back to grab a box next to the XL size *Stud Luvin'* brand of condoms. It made her wonder why those were all locked up too. Maybe to prevent their horribly corny names from escaping and infecting the world?

"Go to counter. I ring you up there."

Obviously pregnancy test were more of a hot commodity than the beer in the open cooler or the cigarettes just out of reach behind the counter. And this was amidst the college campuses. People partied. These rich college kids were responsible. Then again, she was taken to be responsible, being a professional at work and all, and still fell in this awkward limbo. It felt like she owed the woman an explanation or at least to try to plead her case of innocence, but the curt woman rang up the price and Ava was quick to get out of there.

Maybe it was just the slight humiliation or maybe just the need to know, but Ava hurried to the bathroom in the office. The directions were simple, even if she never saw a Rom-Com to know what to do. It was just the wait that was a killer. As she waited, Ava couldn't help but be a little excited.

What if she was pregnant? Jack would make a good father. She had money saved up. Sure it had been for a car, but who really needed a car this close to the city? They had already talked a little about moving in together. All they needed to find was a place with an extra room for the baby. If it was a boy, Ava was sure he'd be as handsome and charming as his father. And a girl would definitely be spoiled.

Ava checked the time on her phone and glanced down at the stick. There was a pink plus sign.

She was pregnant!

Understandably, she was in a bit of a haze as she headed back to her desk. She had to tell Jack! She picked up her phone but decided it would be better to do it in person. After all, he'd be home tomorrow. Sitting down, Ava noticed a note taped to her monitor. It changed everything. Her time had ran out...

Chapter Forty

Jack watched Dunn over his steaming cup of hot chocolate. The man had no idea that now he was the one being watched. There had to be some weakness to exploit. Some way to prove his guilt over killing Ava.

The inspector paced the mezzanine area by the platform stairwells. There was an Acela that would be boarding soon. It must have been one of the trains marked that day for a security check. If Dunn got on that train, his whole day would be a wash and he'd have to try again.

Dunn walked the line of passengers. He didn't even blink twice at a younger woman that could have been a blonde version of Ava, at least the way his mind wanted to see. Nor did he seem to care if they were male or female. Young or old. Wielding a cane or herding small children. Nothing he could use to confront the man about either discrimination or guilt.

"Well played, sir. Well played," he mumbled, taking a sip of his hot chocolate. Jack brooded. The inspector was like an ironclad fortress of secrets.

But then the inspector headed off towards the North Hall. Jack waited a couple seconds before getting up and following. If anything, he could duck over to the elevators as a cover and ride up a floor or two before trying to spy on Dunn again from the building catwalks. So far the inspector was none the wiser.

Jack tossed out his cup before heading into the men's room. He expected to see Dunn at one of the urinals, but all of them were vacant. There was just one stall that had the door closed. Mentally, Jack groaned. Nothing good ever came from a closed door and it wasn't like Jack could really be away from his desk that long. Thinking back, there wasn't anything Dunn ate that would cause a potent stench.

Realizing that he knew the cop's eating habits set him at a new all-time low. With that, Jack took the stall next to the one Dunn was in. He kept his pants up as he took a seat. It was awfully quiet, and he debated if he should be making grunting noises or not. Then again, maybe Dunn had pushed out the big one before he walked in. There really wasn't any abnormal stench from the typical bathroom. And once again, Jack resented the fact that he noted that. Then again, a good spy would, right?

The toilet in the stall next to him flushed, and Jack counted to ten before opening his door to step out. A hand grabbed him by the collar and pinned him against the wall of the stall. Dunn's face was inches from his and those eyes held such a fury that almost made him quiver.

"What the *hell* are you doing?"

That was the big question. Let's see, they were in a bathroom. It should have seemed obvious, but something in that look hinted that he was busted. Yet, Jack couldn't just give up that easily. What proof would the cop have otherwise?

"Had to take a leak."

Dunn laughed, but it was almost worse than the glare. "You must think I'm a damn idiot!"

He opened his mouth to speak, but thought better of it. Jack had enough experience with tricky conversations with Ava to know he was walking into a trap, not that he hadn't just physically walked into a trap.

"This morning, you got a bagel with cream cheese at Au Bon Pain as I got my coffee. You were reading the paper in the mezzanine. An hour later, you were at the police office to get documentation for a parking pass. At lunch you skipped eating with your buddies, got a hot chocolate and followed me into the bathroom."

"So?" There was that sinking feeling.

"You don't grab breakfast in the station. The paper you were reading was two days old and the one the homeless man with the neon green hat used this morning as a bed... and for other things. You do not have a vehicle and the one you attempted to use is a company vehicle and wouldn't need a permit. Then there's the whole following me into the bathroom and lack of action coming from your stall."

The smirk on the man's face was unbearable. He had been caught and Dunn had been on to him from the start.

"So you're stalking me. Don't you cops have something better to do? Maybe-"

"Bullshit," Dunn cut him off. "My job is to observe. I can't help it if I notice a horrible spy wannabe when I see one." He let Jack go and stepped back to rinse his hands. Dunn watched him in the mirror before smirking and grabbing a paper towel. "You're pushing you luck, Jack. This isn't a game. So give up playing spy, hand over everything you have, and forget all about this."

Then he was gone, and Jack was no longer close to getting a break. There was nothing from today that seemed off, let alone criminal, about what Dunn done. There was nothing he could use against him, no proof he was involved in Ava's death or whatever really was going on. Stepping out of the bathroom, Jack anticipated to be pinned again but there was no one around. He turned and headed towards the north end office elevator.

Dunn watched the boy step out. He could tell from the expression on his face that he was frazzled. Luckily, there were no meetings scheduled for today. If Havest had overheard one of those conversations, then this definitely wouldn't be going away. The boy had nothing on him and after today's humiliation, he'd abandon this whole thing and walk away. Havest had the girl's file, so he knew what he had loss. There was no way he'd want to lose even more.

The day felt like a total waste. He had skipped lunch and that bagel from breakfast had barely sufficed. His stomach growled as Jack tried to focus on rail head sections. He could feel himself zoning out when someone knocked on the wall of his cubicle.

"Jack, I think I found something interesting."

He swiveled in his chair to face his buddy. It seemed like since the day he caught him in the bathroom after reading Ava's first note, they had drifted apart. Even now, with going to their group lunches, they really hadn't talked much. It didn't help that Connor's girlfriend stopped by before her shift down at Market East and it made him miss his love even more. Not that Jack could blame his buddy. He was sure that he had been in his own little bubble when Ava was around.

"Really? Two days and you find something?" He groaned. "Con, you have no idea how long I stared at those numbers, and I still have no idea what it all means."

Connor laughed and pulled up the spare chair. He laid out the top couple reports side by side. "Tell me what you see."

His buddy smiled. Clearly, this whole thing had him amused. "I told you, I have no idea."

He shook his head and pointed out three rows of numbers that were identical on both reports. "These here are banking account numbers. The first row is for the corporate account we have in Washington, DC. Now the second two are the accounts the money passed through and where it originated."

Connor flipped to another set of reports. "If we look at these, they're all different. And all the reports use different accounts, except where this all starts and where it ends up." He looked pleased with himself but Jack was still in the dark. What did it really even prove? That someone kept making deposits into their budget and the bank routed things differently each time.

"Connor," Jack sighed, "I'm still not seeing the point. Sure if it was the other way around, but this doesn't make any sense. No alarm bells are going off. No red flags. Hell, if I knew about this sooner, I'd have pushed to order new rail testing equipment or tried to get authorization to go to a couple more conferences last year." Or to have taken someone with him on this last one...

"Doesn't it make you wonder who's sending the money?" Connor leaned back, arms crossed over his chest and looking like the cat that ate the canary. And it did. Each transfer was a couple hundred thousand dollars. It wasn't the kind of money that most people could just toss around at will, and whomever that account belonged to had tossed out close to half a million.

"Depends. Are they still sending money?"

Connor shrugged. "I don't know. You didn't give me those reports, just last year's, and I don't technically work in Accounting. I'm in Payroll." Although he had a gut feeling there was still money coming in. Would a past like this really be worth killing over if it was already done with? "I can tell you that it's coming from someone in DC. Without getting hauled away to a dark interrogation room with a bag over my head, I managed to narrow it down to someone in the Senate."

"So, another dead end." Jack knew there was no way he'd find out who, and what point would that make? There was no way he could go question a congressman. Congressman. Something seemed –

"Guess your spy game's over huh?"

His buddy's words snapped him out of his thoughts. That was the cover story that he had used with Connor – signed up for a spy game as part of the new wave of extreme adventure games. Long forgotten were the days of Civil War reenactments and Murder Mystery dinners. Living out a real spy mission was the real thrill! Or so that's what Connor believed – that Ava had bought them tickets and they were about to expire; ergo, why he was doing it now.

"You're going to have to send me a link to their website. I have to admit, even though you failed, this was pretty cool."

"Con, thanks. You always pull through for me." He didn't correct his buddy's thinking that this was all a simple game. It was far from that.

"That would have meant I saved your ass." Connor shrugged it off and headed out of the cubicle, tossing back a comment that they should hang out this weekend.

Jack watched him leave. He sighed and looked at the reports. There had to be a connection somewhere. Somewhere in Dunn's tax return statements. Someone Dunn was working for. Someone in the Senate. Someone Ava had to have known.

Congressman S. Whitmore.

Chapter Forty-One

"Come on, dude." Connor rolled his eyes. "How can you still be nervous? This is like the eighth store we've been at. Just go in already." He laughed.

But it just wasn't the eighth. It was another store that might have *the one*. Finding the ring was going to make proposing to Ava that much more real. It was one thing to make the dinner reservations. They could just go out to a fancy dinner if he chickened out on proposing. It might make her suspicious of it when they walked in and she saw the place, and she might be a little upset at the end of the night if he didn't. Who was he kidding? Ava wouldn't care. They'd just enjoy themselves and she'd be none the wiser. It wasn't like he wouldn't ask her to marry him... eventually. It was just that Jack started to realize how big this actually was.

"I'm not nervous." Not that his voice was convincing of that fact. "Con, what if I find the ring?"

His buddy chuckled. "Then we're done and can go home. Or at least get something to eat. You promised food would be involved. If I knew you'd starve me for my services, I would have said I was sick or something."

Jack rolled his eyes. "Don't you live for this? You and your girlfriend are always looking at rings. Who better to tell me the difference between a prince cut and a radiant?"

"First off, it's a *princess* cut. And we're not always looking at rings. Lisa is just dropping hints. We finally hit that conversation about marriage and where I see this relationship going."

Connor opened the door and pulled him inside. "We already covered the basics. Silver band. Thin. Size six." He walked along the cases, ruling out things to point out to Jack. "You don't like the pear shape and think the heart cut is too corny."

Jack stopped at one of the smaller display counters as his buddy walked on, rambling on and on about earlier rings.

"See anything you like, sir?"

He looked up and saw the sales associate. A kind smile on the woman's face that matched how light and soft her voice was.

"I'd like to see the second one in the third row."

She opened the back of the case to retrieve the ring. "What's the occasion?"

Jack tried not to laugh. What other reason was there for purchasing a diamond ring? Although, maybe she was just trying to gauge how best to direct the sale. "I'm proposing to my girlfriend."

"She's a lucky lady." The woman handed over the ring and he took it gingerly.

"Wow."

Jack glanced next to him and saw Connor looking over his shoulder.

"That's like, perfectly Ava." He couldn't agree more with his buddy. It was simple, yet far from boring. The diamond wasn't obnoxious, not that he could actually afford one that would come close to those celebrity eye-sores. It had a special sparkle to it. "It's definitely a panty dropper."

And the whole thing was ruined.

"Con!" Jack glared at him. He could see out of the corner of his eye that the sales associate had a similar expression on her face. If he didn't strangle him, she looked insulted enough to do so for him. "That's my future wife you're talking about."

Connor sighed, shaking his head. "Dude, chill."

He nudged the guy away and focused back on the ring. "Could you tell me more about this ring? You know, if it's really an engagement ring or not, how many carats, all the stuff I'm supposed to be asking." It was hard not to feel out of his element.

The woman eyed Connor, who was looking at the earrings while spinning the display carousal, for a moment before looking back to him. She gently laid her hand on his arm.

"It is an engagement ring, and can be a wedding ring also if you're not going to do simple bands at the ceremony." She spoke softly and held eye contact that seemed almost comforting, as if she knew the bundle of nervousness swirling inside him. This was what he had feared. That he had found the one and it would all become real, or something to prevent him from getting it.

"It's a half carat moissanite in a pale rose, almost white, gold setting. Round cut."

"Moissanite?" He had no idea what that was. Was this some way that they were trying to rip him off? Show off a great ring and then it would dissolve in water or something?

"It's growing in popularity with those more ethical concerned over the mining of diamonds. Just as hard and lasting as a diamond, but no blood would ever be spilled over this gem. Prior to the fifties, it could only be found in meteorites. Now, we get a little bit of something special to carry around thanks to white coats in a lab."

Special. That definitely was what he was looking for, and somehow the past of this little stone just fit. Jack took a deep breath, closed his eyes and imagined being on one knee with this ring.

"How do I walk out of here with this ring?" He asked. This was the one. There was no way Ava wouldn't say "yes" when she saw this.

Chapter Forty-Two

Jack realized there was one other person who might know more about these reports. He headed home from work, hoping not to catch them eating dinner. He knocked on the Sandersons' door and waited.

"Coming!"

A moment later, his neighbor's head peeked out of the door. "Jack?"

She seemed just as surprised to see him as he was to realize she might not have just been a bystander, mailing him packages. "Do you have a couple minutes to talk?" He couldn't tell if they were eating and he wasn't sure if that aroma was coming from inside or down the hall. "I'm not interrupting, am I?"

Cora shook her head. "Not really. We were just about to sit down for dinner, but Mikey won't put down his game thing." She rolled her eyes and opened the door. "Why don't you come in? There's enough if you'd like to join us. I made lasagna... and garlic bread."

The invitation was unexpected. So was the prospect of having a delicious home cooked meal again, and lasagna just hit the right buttons. "If you don't mind."

He smiled and stepped inside. The first time he stormed in, Jack hadn't taken in the apartment much. It definitely had a nice homey feeling to it that was both welcoming and overflowing with evidence of a small boy. There was a small row of shoes by the door and Jack took his off, adding them to the end next to the boy's sneakers.

Jack headed towards the kitchen and saw the boy already sitting at the small card table with his plate. A smiled crept over the little face when he walked in. It wasn't like they were best friends but they were at least friendly when they ran into each other. They even talked a little about sports and school stuff on the days he happened to be walking home when the school bus pulled up.

"Oh, let me get those out of the way." Cora rushed pass him as he moved to pull out the third chair. "We usually don't have company." She grabbed the stacks of what looked like old magazines, newspapers, and bills. Jack tried not to laugh, but she clearly caught his expression and blushed.

"Trust me, this is nothing compared to my apartment right now. I never was the tidiest person, and now there's all these reports scattered over everything." It seemed to reassure her enough that it wasn't a personal attack. He took a seat and watched as she took a plate out of the cupboard.

"How big of a piece do you want?" She asked, kitchen flipper in hand.

Jack noticed the smaller servings that were on the boy and her plates. The pile of bills she cleaned off the chair just added to the debate. It wasn't like the apartment was barren, but it was obvious there was something going on. Besides, he was here more to talk and not to eat. There was a Chinese take-out container in the fridge with his name on it.

"Just a small piece is fine. I don't want to get too spoiled by having a real home cooked meal again." He smiled and hoped she would take it as a joke and relieve the slight tension in the room. Maybe that was all just in his mind.

"You can always stop over. Mikey really enjoys talking to you." Cora set the plate down in front of him. "He gets a male role model for a little bit. I have to admit that I'm a little jealous of you."

That shocked him. "What do you mean?"

"You're all he ever talks about when he comes home with you." She gazed over at her boy who was in the middle of cutting off a bite. "He asks for you instead of me. Well, when I have to work and the babysitter comes over it's usually him begging for me to stay. Now I get him pouting over having an old lady instead of you."

"Hey! I don't pout," Mikey chimed in, but there was a hint of a point as the boy crossed his arms and watched them.

"Of course you don't, sweetie. Why don't you eat up before your lasagna gets cold?"

Mikey went back to his plate, but Jack couldn't. "I could babysit. I mean, I've never really babysat before but I've been around kids and I know how to dial 9-1-1."

Cora laughed. "Well, that's good."

She seemed to dismiss the idea; even though Mikey was now paying more attention to their conversation and giving her puppy-dog eyes.

"I'm serious, Cora. I'll watch him a few times for you. We'll have a movie night or we'll be responsible and do homework."

"Pleeeaaassse, mom," Mikey begged.

He chuckled, knowing they were ganging up on her. It wasn't like they were asking to borrow the car and rob a bank or something equally ridiculous and dangerous. It seemed innocent enough and it sounded like something good for them all. The boy's father clearly wasn't around enough and now he'd get to see what it could have been like as a father.

"Jack, I can't pay you. I worked out an arrangement with Mrs. Glophsborn." She shook her head and stared defeated at the plate in front of her.

Was their situation really that bad? Maybe he never paid attention before; but now that he knew, he could understand why Ava helped them behind his back. They needed her and Ava didn't need the guilt he would have given her over not spending that time with him. Had he really been that needy? It seemed like more of a reason to do this now. Ava would have wanted it.

"I didn't ask for money. How about we come to our own arrangement?" Jack smiled and took a bite as he waited to see if she'd consider that.

Her face paled. "I-I don't think I can give you that. I mean, I could but... Mikey and..." She stuttered.

Jack almost choked on the lasagna when he caught on. "I didn't mean sex." He watched relief and then something disheartening pass over her face. "Not that you're not a beautiful woman, but I just lost the love of my life and found out that she was..." It seemed too intimate to let out the little bit of news, even though Ava and the baby were both gone now. He wasn't sure he'd ever tell their families, or if he'd ever be able to find the words. "I was thinking more like getting a home cooked meal once in a while instead." He smiled. "This is really good."

He went back to eating and noticed her relax. Should he have been insulted by her obvious rejection to sleep with him, even if that wasn't his intent? It was more a relief than anything to get their intentions out in the open, but he wondered why they would even have to. Was her situation so complicated? Was there a reason her mind thought to pay with sex first?

"Doesn't his father watch him?" Jack figured it was best to phrase it like that when he didn't see a ring or any photos with a man. If Cora was a lesbian, he didn't want to get off on the wrong foot, not after his earlier enraged visit.

Cora shook her head and he watched as the walls went up again. "I had Mickey right after high school. He didn't want any part of it. Mikey and I got used to things on our own. We like it better this way."

He nodded accepting the idea that she probably didn't want to talk about it, especially with a neighbor. They ate in silence for a while, until the boy cleared his plate and the fork clanked against the ceramic dish. It was probably about time that Jack talked about why he stopped by.

"I got some financial reports," Jack said, dismantling the last bite on his plate.

She perked up and her complete attention was on him. "What reports?" They couldn't be hers. There was no way she could let anyone know they were one bus ticket away from bankruptcy.

"The ones Ava had." He hadn't noticed her reaction as he peeled off another noodle and scrapped off the cottage cheese, then the mozzarella under it. "I had a friend look at them. It seems like someone is sending large amounts to the corporate account, but they transfer it through half a dozen accounts first. And they change the accounts they use each time. He managed to narrow it down to a congressional group, so that's a few hundred."

Cora nodded as she listened and watched him make a mess on the plate. He continued as he reassembled the pasta. "I don't really have proof, but I have a feeling it is Congressman Whitmore. Ava had this VHS tape recording with one of his speeches from the campaign. I thought she had been trying to find something we could talk about and we never did because she..."

Jack took the last messy mouthful. He was trying so hard not to let his mind wander. He had come here to talk about the reports, not Ava. "I think she might have figured it out somehow. She never mentioned knowing you or the babysitting thing, so I have no idea how close you two were... or if she said anything about this?"

"We really didn't talk much about it. Then again, I didn't want to ask any questions. I have learned it is best not to ask sometimes, you know? I had no idea what she was into and I was thinking about my son, Jack. I'm all he's got. I'm sorry."

Cora got up and collected the emptied plates. Had he really expected her to know anything? He watched her as she stood at the sink, doing the dishes. "Naw, I understand. I'm just coming to a dead end and grasping at straws." He sighed.

"Well do you know who Ava could have talked to? I mean, if she knew what those reports said, wouldn't she had left a note or something? I didn't really know her but, if she put all this together and the other things seemed written out, it seems like she would have wrote it out for you."

She had a point. He had been thinking that Ava knew or had the key to deciphering the numbers. Connor seemed clueless, if he had been the one to help her figure this all out before. It was like he never saw the reports at all. He was the only one in their circle of friends with financial knowledge, and Jack couldn't recall her mentioning anyone in her family that would fit the bill.

"I wasn't really around much when all this was going on." A guilty feeling started to creep up. If he was, could all of this been avoided? Would Ava have worked this all out with him and they'd be happily engaged with a baby on the way? "Unless she found someone new, I don't think so. I've tried to think of people we knew, and I can't think of anyone who would know their way around these numbers."

Cora just nodded and tucked the dishes away in the rather empty cupboards. He had been expecting some words of wisdom, but apparently he'd be left wanting.

"So why do you think it's Whitmore?" She asked, sitting across from him at the table.

"He was on the tape Ava left."

"That's it? No tingling sensation or psychic vision?"

Jack chuckled. "No, none of that."

"Then why? Maybe she really was just trying to talk politics with you or maybe he's one of the good guys."

There was merit to what Cora was saying. He had just assumed guilt. There were no scandals in the news. Nothing unusual other than the one interview that Ava managed to capture. Had he been completely wrong about this guy because of a clip a couple minutes long?

"I guess not then." Jack shrugged.

"Wrong." She smiled and leaned back in the chair. "It's definitely him. There's just something off about him and his politics. Like, how he's so anti-drug and strict gun control, but then let's these mob guys walk. Well, I don't know if they're actually mob guys, but they're not good news."

Jack let that sink in a little. It sounded way too much like those spy and mystery stories that were all the rage when he was growing up. Ava could almost fit the whole Russian spy stereotype. Well, at least in his fantasies about skintight black suits and uber flexibility she did fantastically. But that was something that he couldn't think about right now.

"Just speaking out loud and hypothetically," he started. Jack laced his fingers and propped his elbows up on the table. "Whitmore could be involved with drug and gun, um, trafficking?" It was a long stretch but seemed plausible to those quick thrill story lines. "If the money's coming from him, then those numbers have to be a payoff."

"So there's someone going all the grunt work while he looks like an angel. But how does that fit in with the money going into your budget?"

That was the million dollar question, quite literally. "I don't know. There's no way that it could have gotten to a certain person without the watchdogs hunting this person down and kidnapping them off the street." Okay, so he was living his childhood fantasies for a moment longer. "I'm not sure it could even get to a specific department or group. That would mean there's a mole or someone in the company routing it, and I can't see that happening."

And just like that, it seemed their little story was dead in the water. It all sound good on paper, but it fell apart in the real world.

"Well, couldn't it be going to a certain project? Amtrak just was in the newspaper about this tunnel thing into New York. It's going to take years and it said some of the money was from grants. Those get channeled just to that, right?"

He nodded. "I didn't think about that. I guess it could be set up like that. Whoever is working with Whitmore would just charge their work to some accounting number. They might get away with it but, Cora, this has been going on for years. I'd like to think if something this shady was going on that they'd be caught by now."

"Yea, me too," she said quietly.

Chapter Forty-Three

Jack turned the television on as he got ready in the morning. It seemed that lately there was such a void of camaraderie in his life that the bit of noise from the box helped ease it. If only a little. It definitely made the apartment seem homier.

He showered and changed, taking his time to make sure that he looked put together. Connor finally told him how frazzled he had looked lately. Maybe he should have expected it. This whole case, not that he had anything better to call what Ava left him, seemed almost finished until that one dead end. But now, he was back to feeling so close to solving it.

"Local authorities arrested three last night on the Keystone headed towards Harrisburg, Pennsylvania. It is believed that the three men are part of an emerging heroin and cocaine trafficking ring linked to the greater Philadelphia area."

Jack paused. Had he heard that right? There was something going on with their trains? He pushed down the bread in the toaster and walked out to the living room to turn up the morning news.

"The bust came from a fellow passenger who called in a tip about 'suspicious activity' in the last car of Train 693 that was the last scheduled departure for Harrisburg from 30th Street Station. There have been suspicions that traffickers were using mass transit. This bust is the third this year and the largest seized. Officers seized thousands of dollars cash along with cocaine and heroin. Raising security on transit routes is currently in talks. An increase in the use of drug-detecting canines is one of the implementations that we can expect to see in the short-term."

It was a strange coincidence, but it had to be just that. Dunn's confrontation was only that. It just happened and the cop probably had been worried about breaking that news to him. After all, it wasn't like he had taken having a file with graphic photos and a medical report saying his girlfriend was pregnant exactly well.

Although, what if there was another reason Dunn was acting differently. It wasn't like he could talk to him again to try to persuade him to give up. Maybe it was just a side effect of last night's talk, but what if this was connected? Maybe the money was coming in to fund these drug trafficking. The money had to be going to some illegal activities if it was being kept such a quiet secret. Then again, if it was such a quiet secret, how would have Ava known? He was just making desperate grasps in thin air. Although something seemed to nag his mind. This seemed oddly familiar.

The toast popped up, causing him to jump. He almost had let it all consume him again. Jack sighed and grabbed the peanut butter out of the cupboard. He dug around in the jar with the knife to smear a good helping on each slice. Why did it seem familiar though? It was like he knew all along, but it bothered him so much that he couldn't completely enjoy his guilty breakfast.

He shoved the last bit of the slice in his mouth as he turned off the television. It had moved onto the weather and he really didn't want to know how horrible it was going to be tomorrow. Jack knew he'd focus more on how to get out of work the next day than working on his projects. But there was just something about the Harrisburg Line that kept lingering in the back of his head. Jack grabbed his jacket and coffee. He headed out the door, trying to focus on work right now. If not, he was going to be late getting in.

Jack sat down at the table with his friends at lunch. It felt nice, having gotten back into the routine, and it no longer felt forced. It was just that now so many more theories floated around his head and he couldn't even slip them into the conversation. These people were their friends, but Ava had worked with a couple of them on some of her projects. What if they were connected to whatever she got into? What if Dunn, and whomever he worked for, had someone on the inside within their group? It was a rather big, and doubtful, risk.

"Dude, you okay?"

He glanced up from his tuna melt. Well, his attempt at a tuna melt. After all the hot meals Cora made as babysitting payments, he had craved more food that wasn't microwaved or frozen. It was just that his cooking skills were so rusty that he was risking his life eating it now.

"Just this project. It's kicking my ass right now." Jack just shrugged at his friends' chuckles. They all knew how things went. One day you're twiddling your thumbs, playing Solitaire on the computer, and the next you're skipping lunch and staying hours late trying to finish something.

He took a tentative bite of the sandwich. If risking his health was so easy, how much greater was the cost to ask a question? If he could think of an innocent one maybe it would reveal if any of them were on the other side.

"Has anyone else had cops show up at their field projects?"

Confused looks met him all around the table. At least it wasn't just a strange notion in his mind. It appeared this definitely wasn't normal behavior.

"No." Connor leveled his gaze. "What did you do?"

A nervous laugh escaped him. "I did nothing! It's just that they showed up on the Harrisburg Line upgrades. We're still a little short in my department, so they volun-told me to check it out to make sure we're on track."

Why had he bothered to ask? Obviously it was a bad idea. It just brought up something Ava related and maybe tipped them off that he was digging into her work, snooping. It had just seemed like it was one of the key pieces into solving this thing.

"I've never had them just show up. Well, there was that one time we were working nights and some of the neighbors complained about the noise. An Amtrak cop just drove by, saw it was us and probably went to grab a donut or cup of coffee."

"You're right about that - if they get calls or have to keep the public away." Connor sat back and listened to his friends. "Remember that time the track equipment busted a hose and gallons of oil got all over the place. I heard it got in the water, some pond or something, and killed a bunch of bugs and some fish. So these environmental nuts show up to protest and stop work. Saw something on the news about them being there for that."

"Yea, never just showing up for the hell of it. What upgrades were you doing, Jack? Anything "bad"?"

He laughed as the girl from the Finance group used air quotes. "No, just normal stuff. Track upgrades... new switches... fresh ballast and ditching..."

It didn't make any sense. Upgrades were normal everywhere on the system and, yet, it seemed like the cops only cared about the Harrisburg line. What could possibly make that route special?

Jack sighed and suffered through the rest of his dry tuna melt. His mind drifted back to the news that morning. Harrisburg Line. Drugs. *Mafia.* And why would they care about track upgrades? The only out of the ordinary thing was the ballast renewal and... Jack couldn't believe it.

He jumped up from the table, throwing his trash away as he dashed away. The comments of his friends at his sudden, strange behavior never registered. Ava would have wondered why the cops were always at her projects. She would have dug and she had found the answer. He just needed to see those photos she left to make sure.

There were *bodies*.

Chapter Forty-Four

Thorpe watched his partner pace the length of their office. This definitely wasn't good. That drug bust on the Keystone was just one more failure on their plate. Well, Dunn's. He was the lead on this. He was the one that made all the contact and had all the connections.

"They're going to be calling, and what the hell am I going to tell them?"

"That it wasn't our fault? They can't expect us to control what these passengers do. Out of all the runs they want, they can't expect things to go perfectly every time."

Dunn stopped pacing. "That's exactly what they're expecting! That's what they're paying us to ensure, Thorpe."

He started to pace again, trying to come up with a way out of this. First that girl, then her idiot boyfriend and now drug busts. He had vowed to do everything exactly so those mafia henchmen never returned to his home, and now it felt like a done deal. There was no way that they'd just sit around idle and make phone calls. Maybe the big boss in Washington, DC would but not these guys.

"Dunn, sit down. You'll give yourself a heart-attack worrying about this and I can't stand your pacing."

He sighed and plopped down into his chair. "What am I going to tell my wife if things go south and they come after us? She's not going to pack up and leave her book club… or knitting circle."

"Who says you need to tell her anything?"

Dunn humpf'd. As if he could get away with that. His partner had no idea what married life really was like. It wasn't like the girlfriends Thorpe kept. There was no way his wife, who knew him well enough to make the decisions he wanted before he knew he wanted them, could be fooled by a lie, even a small one.

"Okay, so if they come, why don't you blame it on Havest? Say it's his fault and let them take care of kid. I know the boss remembers the girl and if you tell him the boyfriend is snooping, they'll realize we had other problems to deal with."

"Yea, let one stupid kid who no one would believe take precedence over a thousand dollar drug run. Right…" Dunn got up. "They'd kill us for being idiots, then go after the boy."

He headed towards the office door. "I need a beer, but a coffee's going to have to do. You want me to get you something?"

Thorpe just shook his head. "No, but you're making me wonder if I should ask for your gun. I can picture you going on a shooting spree 'bout now."

Dunn didn't deny that the idea sounded good. At least he could make a real attempt to get rid of Havest, but he doubted he'd be so lucky to find the schmuck in the mezzanine. He headed out into the station, playing out the idea in his head, knowing it was something he'd never do.

Thorpe walked in, holding his face. "Those fuckers found me last night. Came at me on the streets outside my girl's place." He sat down across from Dunn in the office. "They said beating your old ass wasn't enough of a persuasion when it would probably kill you."

He groaned while Dunn sipped his coffee. "Guess for once, it pays to be older."

"Not by much." Thorpe goes to grab a bottled water from the mini-fridge to hold to his bruised and busted lip. That looks to be the worst of the beating, but these gangster wouldn't go so easy when they're hyped up on money loss anger. They probably had orders to limit the amount of visible damage while he was in uniform, make him less conspicuous.

"So, what did you tell them?"

Thorpe grumbled and stole half of Dunn's apple cinnamon muffin. "Just that we were dealing with a security threat." He nibbled the stolen goods. "I couldn't tell them it was the boy, not that they gave me time to before punching my moneymaker."

He rolled his eyes. Sometimes his partner acted like a child over the way he valued looks. "So they don't know about Havest?"

"Naw, not yet and I'm not wanting to be the one telling them. We were supposed to have taken care of the problem with the girl. Tellin' 'em would just be telling 'em we failed. I ain't taking more of a beating for that when I can avoid it."

Dunn took a long drink from his mug. The mafia might not know, yet, that was the only good news. They needed to fix this problem – and soon – so that when the mafia did hear about it, they could claim it never happened because the alleged issue was handled.

"So what we going to do 'bout the boy? Take him and give him over to the guy like we were going to with that girl? Push him in front of a train? Bury the body under that new track out west?"

"We can't do anything to the boy. If some homicide cop comes snooping, they'd follow the trail back to us and then piece it together with the girl's death. That be the surest way to ensure our deaths." Dunn stared at his coffee, hoping the magical liquid that kept him awake could solve this problem as well.

"We're going to have to make it look like a suicide. I gave him the girl's file. He should be torn up about it. Maybe so much so to take his own life." He couldn't help but smile. Havest hadn't back down and it seemed like his last attempt to save the boy would become his ending.

"Home visit?" Thorpe asked, scooting forward now that they moved onto something more interesting and less painful than his face. "I got a buddy who can find us an unregistered piece. Probably a Glock. Those are his favorite."

Dunn nodded. "We'll start making the plans. After you get the gun, we'll pay him a little visit. There's a few possessions left in evidence from the investigation." He got up and walked over to the file cabinet that held employee records. "We're going to have to do a little digging to make sure this doesn't blow up in our faces again."

Chapter Forty-Five

Jack stood in the corner of the Post Office. His hands were shaking a little as he made a copy of everything. It was costing a small fortune, but it had to be done. He needed a back-up plan. Ava had one; albeit, it was elaborate. He just needed someone else to hold the secrets in case something happened to him, or the originals.

It was hard not to think that the buy-out option would have been better to take. There would be no crazy cops coming after him or prying into his life. There's be no horrifying reality of not only the company, but the government as well. But changing his decision would have cost him what felt like extra time with Ava. All those times he thought she was right there, laughing at him, cheering him on... and then learning Ava was pregnant, her last secret. It was so worth it.

He slid the copies into the large manila envelope and grabbed a blank sheet out of the machine. The records could only lead someone to the money funneling from someone high up in political bullshit and surrounded by impenetrable walls, someone protected. The other side of the coin needed a more direct and spelled out connection for whoever may see these papers after him.

Congressman Whitmore grew up in North Philly and made mafia connections. He funds a reimbursable government project to improve the Harrisburg line. Only police has access to those project numbers. Police make sure no one finds the mafia hits buried. Improved track will lead to better rides and increased service. It'll make drug trafficking easier and they can move more. Dunn got paid off shortly after joining the Amtrak force. He killed Ava...

Jack stared at his sketchy writing. He slid the sheet in with the rest and slowly exhaled. Somehow, it felt like a huge weight was taken off his chest. Somehow, it was all going to work out. Somehow, eventually, it was going to be alright.

Dunn just sat there at the table outside the coffee shop in the station. He looked so normal and oblivious to everything going on. The man didn't look as evil as he had discovered the cop to be. Had this been the same way he saw Ava? Just a girl with a normal life, an easy target?

There was no way the old man would be prepared for this. It was as blindsiding of an attack as was Ava's death.

Jack took a few deep breaths. He couldn't go in half-assed or nervous. He had to be confident and make Dunn believe he knew exactly what he was saying, and have the proof to back it up. He needed to make sure exactly who was behind this. He needed the proof. He needed the words his cell phone could record.

"Dunn, I know everything." He stood in front of the man.

The man tried to blow him off, getting up and walking away. "I have no idea what you're talking about, boy."

Jack followed after him as he walked towards the concourse. "I know you're working for Congressman Whitmore. I know that you're helping these drug traffickers." That got the man to stop. "You're also keeping us from accidentally finding mob hits too. I'm going to let it all out."

His breath left in an instant as Dunn pinned him against the wall. "You maggot!"

He tried to pull the old man's hands from his neck, but they just squeezed tighter. Jack had underestimated the cop's strength and it was going to cost him. Every breath got more labored.

"Hey!"

Dunn released him and he slide down to the floor, coughing and trying to catch his breath. The passenger that had interrupted them, thankfully, came over.

"You okay, mister? Want me to call the *real* police?"

Jack looked to the older guy with a red roller bag. He shook his head and got up. Even if the passenger didn't call, someone else who might have seen could, and that was exactly what he should be doing. If Dunn was pushed so far that he'd snap here in public, then his act had gone too far and his life was really at risk now. He had to end this before it ended him.

Chapter Forty-Six

He walked out of the nondescript building that occupied the 600 block of Arch Street. Dunn couldn't believe it. He thought it was some kind of sick joke. First it was a call from Congressman Whitmore, himself. Then it was their agent at the Bureau calling to tip him off that someone was onto them.

You'd think that idiot Havest would have learned! Obviously that warning a week ago meant nothing. Dunn had been so sure that he got through to the boy. His face had paled at the information and photos, and it seemed like that threat had been alleviated. Even a few photos, and finding out he could have been a father, should have drove the point home to Havest that these people were serious about keeping up with their secrets. Did the death of that girl mean nothing to him?

That idiot was going to get them both killed. It was too bad that Dunn was a little attached to living. As he was walked up Arch Street, that's when it changed – the brown-haired mess wandered away, not quite a block ahead of him, in a navy peacoat. There wasn't another soul on the street. No one to witness anything, and he still had a job to do. Dunn pulled out his concealed ebony Kel-Tec PF-9 from his side holster.

He was going to make sure it ended today. Dunn planted his feet and took aim. The sight of the pistol trained on the back of that messy head of hair. He popped off the safety and took two deep breaths to calm his nerves. A shot like this could be ruled as accidental gang fire, like Havest was mistaken for someone else. It was too far away to be executioner style, so there wasn't going to be such a search for a motive and bettered Dunn's chance to get away scotch-free.

His finger ran over the trigger. Two minutes and his life would be perfect again – one to shoot Havest and the other to getaway. It was then that the boy stopped. Dunn watched as he got ready to cross the street and glanced back, checking for traffic. A pair of emerald eyes widened. Dunn fired off a shot and barely missed as the boy dashed across the street and disappeared.

"Shit!"

Dunn dropped the gun to his side as he ran after the boy. The worst part was not having eyes on him yet; but when he got to the corner, he saw Havest. He raised the gun to fire off another shot, but Havest turned a corner. The boy was still the length of a block ahead and he cursed, having let himself slip out of prime shape. The only thing was to guess where Havest would go and to cut him off.

The reasonable escape route was the subway. They were on 8th Street and one stop was just a short way ahead on Market Street, but that would have left Havest in his line of fire. One disadvantage was that they both lived here long enough to know the layout of downtown. Havest had taken Filbert. To cut him off, he had to take another route to bet him to the 11th Street Station. The problem was to do that, Dunn would have to run down another block and up Market, the most crowded street, filled with tourists. There was no way he'd make it through the people, let alone unnoticed with a gun.

It was still a crapshoot. Havest could disappear underground at the Market Street entrance or The Gallery mall entrance, slipping over to the subway or a SEPTA train. The latter would be the worse. Dunn's best shot was taking Arch Street until 11th and getting an eye on both.

He turned the corner onto 11th Street and ran down, keeping close to the building. Filbert was just feet in front of him and traffic, what little there was, was flowing in the opposite direction and giving him the advantage of knowing if a vehicle was turning to slow him. Dunn was about to cross when he fell on his back at the corner of the building with a pain in his head from something hitting him.

The gun had slipped from his hand, but it wasn't lost. It was right in his face, and Havest was behind it. Many guns had been pointed at him in his career and many of the wielders were going to pull the trigger. He was positive that Havest wanted to pull that trigger. The look in the boy's eyes were like none he ever saw in them before. He looked wild. He looked ready to kill.

"What are you going to do? Shoot me?" Dunn chuckled. He was a logical man and probably would have seen through the inspector's hostile tact. The only hope was to disarm the boy with the emotions that must be stirring inside. Havest just relived everything. It had to be all fresh in his mind.

"You ruined my life." The gun shook slightly in Havest's hands. It was obvious that emotions were there. "You took Ava from me. You tried to kill me!"

The boy was not keeping it together at all. Maybe using this tact was more dangerous than trying to talk him down. Dunn knew he couldn't wait much longer and shifted slightly.

"Don't move!" Havest growled out. The gun was still focused on him, but now his chest – a larger target. Even if the boy never held a gun before, which Dunn was betting was true, it was going to be hard to miss. "You ruined my life. Now I'm going to ruin yours."

Havest kept the gun trained on him and he waited for the trigger to be pulled. Instead, the boy moved one hand to grab his cell phone from a back pocket.

"Kieran, it's Jack Havest. I need you to come to Market East Station." Havest's glare and tremor in his trigger finger kept Dunn in place. Any move from the nervous wreck might accidentally discharge. If only he had put the safety back on and not been so eager for the kill shoot. The boy would have never realized it and could have been taken down.

"Dunn had a gun. Shot at me. I... I have him here." Dunn watched as the boy hung up and tucked his cell phone away.

"Jack, listen to me. You have no idea what you're doing. Let me go. I'll tell them you're dead. You can get away, start a new life. Disappear." Not that he really was going to let that happen. It would seal both their deaths instantly.

Havest just slowly shook his head and didn't move. Sirens were coming and he knew this was going to be bad. That meant cops. Cops that both knew him and didn't. People that were both part of this and who weren't. People who wanted to ensure his silence.

Dunn glared back up at the boy as two FBI agents appeared to arrest him. He recognized one as a man who strolled out of Havest's little meeting, and he was the one to read him the Miranda Rights while shoving him towards the back of a unmarked car that flashed blue and red lights.

"This isn't over, Havest! You fucked up!" He yelled over his shoulder and he was pushed in the back, having the door slammed behind him. Dunn glared out at the boy on the street. The boy hadn't moved a muscle and the gun was still trained on the spot he had fallen. Havest froze, but he could tell that tears drained out. If nothing else, Dunn had the satisfaction to know he had broken the boy.

Chapter Forty-Seven

"Son of a bitch!" Whitmore paced his office. He'd just gotten off the phone with his lawyers. Things were blowing up in his face. Everything ran without a hitch for decades and now, suddenly, no one could keep their shit together.

"Jeanne, connect me to Wakefield in Toronto." He left his finger slip off the intercom button as he continued to wear a hole in his floor. The only thing he could ever count on was money. He should have known better than to try to save a buck.

It took less than a minute for his secretary to patch him through. "Sir?"

"I'd like to entertain your cousin. I believe I said that I'd owe you the favor if he ever came to Philadelphia." The Congressman felt a little stress flee. This was the man he should have used to get rid of that damn nosy bitch. Even though he knew his phones were tapped now and everything was piling up against him, no one could stop him.

"Marco will be pleased. He'll be there tomorrow." Whitmore smiled as he hung up. He should have felt something. After all, he'd be next to the man when he was going to be shot. The court hearing tomorrow was going to brighten his day.

Whitmore powered down his computer and grabbed his suit jacket off his coat rack. "I'm leaving early, Jeanne. Please hold my calls and clear tomorrow's schedule. I'm sure our friends at the FBI plan on keeping me the day and I don't want their hospitality to reflect poorly on this office." He spoke eloquently as he crossed the room.

"Also, call Congressman Jutgers and have him re-schedule our business meeting for next week." With that, he was out the door.

It didn't even take a full day. By nightfall, the FBI had pulled Dunn's records. They saw that the Congressman phoned him, as well as an agent at the Bureau. Both were being taken in for questioning. Their call histories seemed to only further cement the accusations that Havest had made.

By the end of that week, four random raids on the train route sponsored by the Congressmen saved six young girls being trafficked and took in over half a million worth in various drugs. One less corrupted politician was in Washington DC and one less disgraceful officer was on the streets. Nabbing the mafia members was harder, but it was definitely progressing.

Jack stood on the platform. He knew that he needed to get out of town and the FBI agent was growing short on patience. But he couldn't leave her just yet. This platform – it was the last place Ava had stood. It looked so ordinary for having such a hold upon him. It had all started in this station. They met in this place, he laughed with her here, fell in love with her here. This spot was where their first adventure started. This spot was where it all ended.

He glanced up when he heard the regional train coming into the station. That was the last thing she ever saw. It was a sad realization, but he was learning to let that go. Ava would always be in his heart and with him forever.

"I love you, Ava. Forever and always."

Chapter Forty-Eight

Ava shut off the computer. Everything was set and out of her hands. All, except one thing.

Jack.

His train was due soon; and according to train status online, it was going to arrive on time. Everything depended on it being no more than two minutes late. She knew they were coming today. She had seen that man downstairs and knew it was over. They weren't going to let her be bought off. Apparently, the powers at play thought she was too much of a risk.

She headed towards the stairwell. It would take her straight down to the mezzanine. Then it would be only a quick dash down the stairs to the train platform. It was still riskier than the elevators. Ava may have more escape routes along the way in the stairwell, but she was in the open. Anyone could walk in to travel between floors or peer down and see her. If it was Dunn or another officer, it would be all over. The worst part was Ava didn't know who else could be in on this. All she had was just one dangerous piece of information and the name of the man doing the footwork.

The stairwell was empty when she started the descent from the fourth floor. But as she passed the door to the second, above her one slammed shut. Then there were footsteps coming down. Sure, it could have been anyone, but who would be doing down quickly if not to run or catch someone?

Ava stuck to the outside of the stairwell, losing precious seconds but remaining hidden. When her hand touched the back of the mezzanine level door, there was no ounce of relief in her. Whoever entered the stairwell had closed the gap to maybe a single flight of stairs.

The food court seating area was packed when she emerged. As she bolted for the building's center for the stairs to platform level, she almost collided with an elderly woman. Age was one fear that was going to be deprived of her if the plan didn't work.

She risked a glance back and the blood drained from her face some. Dunn and another officer were only yards behind her. The only thing aiding her now was her age and health as she sprinted.

People she darted around just glanced her way before going about their business. She needed to be remembered more than a possible homeless woman fleeing police custody, although she was dressed far from that. Ava pushed over a potted plant, supposedly to beautify the station, as she passed. She bumped into as many travelers as she dared without slowing her too much. Her heart was pounding as she shouted and begged for help.

It was like a crowded sea of faces until the Solari flip board of train arrivals and departures was upon her. Breaking into that sudden open space almost sent her tumbling on her face. But she needed stairwell number five. She knew that's where Jack's train would be. She needed to get to him first.

Ava didn't hear anyone coming down those stairs after her. But it was only a matter of time. There were people who saw her and cameras trained on the passages that someone in a small, dark room was probably watching and snitching on her. She ducked behind a pillar.

In her head, she went over the plan again. Find Jack in the crowd, most likely in the last car or two unless he decided to break his habit. Which if he did, she already swore to haunt him every moment of his life. But, find Jack. Get him back onto the train. She had debated every hiding place possible, but there was only one. Somehow, in a matter of seconds, she needed to pull her boyfriend into the bathroom, bar the door closed and hope the light indicating it was occupied did not display. If only Ava kept her cell to just find him or say goodbye. No, she couldn't think about saying goodbye. Not to Jack. Not now or ever.

There were voices. Passengers wouldn't have been allowed down here this early. Ava moved around the pillar to keep it between her and whoever was coming. They stopped right on the other side of her pillar.

"She's down here, Marshall. The cameras caught her. Keep looking." Slowly, the breath she hadn't realized she was holding leaked out. Somehow, she needed to get pass two men, both larger than her.

The train's bell was chiming as it crept into the station. If she could put enough distance between them before the passengers started to exit, then there might be just enough time to get Jack and hide without being caught. And then the train would be continuing its way up to New York City. They'd get off and disappear into the bustle of the super-city, maybe stay with a friend for a couple days until they had a plan.

Ava counted to ten in her head. She took off, running the opposite direction of the train travel, towards it. All she had to do was make it a couple hundred feet down the platform and wait for the train to stop to be at the end. But she felt something grab her arm.

"Not so fast!" It was Dunn. The other man was only a few feet behind him. She tried to pull the older man along, but he was too heavy and time was running out. Ava begged him to let her go as she worked on prying off his fingers. She stumbled backwards a little when his grip finally released. The only thing stopping her from slipping into the path of the oncoming train was the yellow rumble strip along the edge of the platform.

She caught herself and started down the platform. The train was blowing its horn, unsure of what would happen in the next few moments. There wasn't going to be a getaway. There wasn't going to another embrace or a smile or anything from Jack again. There wasn't going to be a life with her in it where they were perfectly happy and safe. Tears streamed down her face as her thoughts tripped her up. Her body was falling again. All that was left was the light at the end of the tunnel.

I love you, Jack. Forever and always.

If Life Was Different

Jack paced outside of La Famiglia on Front Street. Tonight was the night. He was actually going to do it. There were going to be no more cold feet moments. No more nights regretting he couldn't find the perfect moment. The perfect moment was going to happen when Ava says "yes" tonight. That was the only moment that was going to be worth anything in his life.

He checked his watch, again. Seven thirty-five. Their reservation was for eight, but nerves got him there an hour early. The restaurant knew what he had planned. Everything was going to go perfectly. But then why was he so nervous?

Ava had been with him for over three years. They spent all their time together. They were happy. She loved him. How could he even humor the idea that she'd reject him?

He sighed and decided to head inside. Their table was perched at the back of the restaurant, next to the window where they'd watch the boats drift across the Delaware River. That was if they bothered to look away from each other, or this restaurant. It was his first time actually inside the place and it was more beautiful than from the passing glance on the street. The soft chandelier lighting was a wonderful accent that lit the paintings and treasures from Italy so well.

Jack sat down, facing the door. He had already placed their order when he called last night to check on their reservation he booked weeks ago. Ava would her arancini to nibble on while the chef wiped up their main course. He hoped that maybe she'd share those little fried rice balls after getting distracted by the ring on her finger.

The waiter brought a plate of bread and oil to the table as he checked his watch again. The nerves were starting to act up again. What if she couldn't find the place? What if she wasn't coming at all? What if she...

"Hey, babe."

She was gorgeous.

Her hair was pulled up in a loose bun while a few rebellious curls escapes and framed her face. Jack got up to pull the chair out for her, wanting to beat the waiter to do it. He didn't want another man close to her tonight, not when every eye had to be on her and he wanted to be the only one to hold hers.

"You look beautiful, Ava."

He sat across from her. The flicker of the candlelight made her eyes sparkle. How was he ever going to be able to tear himself away for a moment to propose?

She laughed softly. "You don't look so bad yourself. I can't believe you've been hiding this sexy Jack from me the whole time," Ava teased.

What that girl didn't do to him! She made every doubt and all his nerves disappear. They were perfect for each other and tonight everyone else would know that.

"Awfully fancy place." Ava looked around, her eyes lingering on a knickknack or two. "Are we celebrating or something?"

She must have thought it was work related. The project he slaved on for years was finally getting off the ground and starting to take shape. It was a big step, career-wise for Jack. But that wasn't the reason for why the waiter brought over two flutes of champagne.

"Definitely 'or something'." Jack smiled as the sight of the glasses confused her more. Somehow his plan hadn't slipped out, and it was so hard to keep secrets from her. At least the really good ones.

Ava turned the glass with her fingers while he took a sip. "Fancy restaurant. Champagne."

Was she going to figure it out? Every romance story gave away what was coming next. Maybe he should have gone more original. But if he thought there was any risk to her spoiling the surprise it was gone when the arancini came out.

"Okay, now I definitely know what's going on." She smirks. "You get me to come to a fancy restaurant in a dress. Bring me champagne, arancini." Ava leans closer and lowers her voice. "You want to have sex tonight."

She stabs a ball with her fork and takes a suggestive bite. Then she licks her lips without breaking eyes contact until she winks and sits back. "Babe, it's a given. You didn't have to do all this. Although I'm glad you got the balls."

Jack watched her go for another one. His hand slipped into his pocket. This was it. He was ready, if not momentarily confused and turned on by her. Jack moved to push his chair back when the main course arrived and shattered his confidence. Ava hadn't seemed to notice. She was enjoying the night too much and he wished that he could just let the restaurant do what they were going to do and relax. He reached for the flute and took a sip to calm his nerves. He'd get a chance to ask after dinner; that was all.

He watched Ava unfold her napkin and lay it on her lap. Maybe ordering a red sauce pasta dish was a horrible idea. It could ruin the light pink chiffon. The thin-strapped dress looked too beautiful on her to wish its death by an errant noodle.

Jack knew he should be eating and enjoying their night out as well, but all he could do was reach again for the liquid courage that tickled as it ran over his tongue.

"Ava, you should try the champagne. It's really good." He had noticed her glass remained full. She had eyed it when it arrived at their table, toyed with the stem of the glassware, but hadn't actually taken a sip yet. "It has a nice fruity taste, more like strawberries."

Her face dropped a little as she looked to the glass. "I don't want any champagne. I mean, I can't."

"You can't?" Jack was confused. Why couldn't she? It wasn't like Ava never drank. She wasn't much of a drinker, but one glass with dinner wasn't something he thought she'd turn away from. Maybe she really had figured out what tonight was about and the champagne was him, and she was rejecting him.

"I, um," she started. Her face blushed a little as her hands fidgeted in her lap. "Jack, I'm pregnant," she said quietly.

Pregnant? He couldn't have heard that right. There was just that one time after Connor's Halloween party. If she was pregnant... Oh god, did she cheat on him?

Jack hated himself the second that thought passed through his mind. There was no way Ava would do that to him, and he knew she hadn't. They were together almost all the time. It made him wonder why they even bothered with two apartments, when one of them was never at home.

"I'm pregnant, Jack." She said a little more confident. "I took a pregnancy test last week and went to my doctor." Ava glances up, searching his face for any clue of what's going on in his mind. "I... we're going to have a baby. I mean, that is, if you still want to be with me... and the baby."

Her voice started to get a little shaky and the next thing Jack knew he was kneeling down next to her. "Shh, Ava. Don't even think something like that."

The look on her face had said it all. Ava had thought having a baby was going to drive him away. There was no way she could give up or kill their baby. Her mind had started with the worse and made her buy into it, even for a moment. It was just a fear, not a doubt that she had of his love for her. But if it came down to it, she'd be with the baby. A baby that had a little piece of both of them.

"Ava, I love you. And I'm going to love our baby." He smiled softly.

He was already in the right position and his was entwined with hers. If that moment of fear hadn't passed over her face, it would have been perfect. That moment may have passed but he had a chance to make the next one theirs.

Jack slipped his hand into his jacket pocket and pulled out the small velveteen box. "Ava Koltrin," he smiled, "I have loved you since the moment you were forced to sit in my cubicle for your crash course of Amtrak. I have loved you every time you forgot to put the milk back in the fridge and every time you accuse me of being the one who snores." She laughed a little.

"I don't want to fall asleep another night without you in my arms or wake up without your frizzy bedhead next to me. I want to spend every day making you fall in love with me over and over again. I want to spend the rest of my life with you, and our little baby."

He popped open the box and watched as her eyes grew wide at the sight of moissanite ring that matched the hue of her dress. Her eyes were starting to glisten with the threat of tears. "Will you marry me?"

Her lips found his and the world disappeared. Nothing else mattered in that moment, except one thing. When they finally were fighting for a breath, Jack asked again, never letting his lips linger far from hers.

"Yes! Of course I'll marry you." She kissed him again as he slid the ring on her finger.

Jack paced in the antechamber of the church. His nerves were getting the best of him but, at least being Saturday morning, he didn't have to wait long for Ava to become his wife. That was the only good thing about this, after last night of tossing and turning alone.

"Jack, they're here."

Connor laughed and walked over after seeing his face. "Jack, don't worry. She said yes to you once. You haven't done anything stupid since, right?"

"Oh god, she's not going to marry me!"

His best man just laughed and smacked him on his back. "I promise I won't let her escape the church until she marries you. Deal?"

"Deal." Jack groaned as he headed towards the door to walk onto the alter. "I just hope you're careful. She likes to bite."

"I'm not worried about her." Connor shook his head and followed him out to their places alongside the priest.

The small church was relative packed. Both of their families had come and almost all of their friends from work too. It wasn't the fact that every person he cared about was sitting here, waiting to hear what Ava's answer would be. It was the start of the music that made his nervous. The maid of honor walked down and then she stepped out. And Jack felt like the wind was knocked out of him.

Her short white wedding gown almost matched the little girl's dress, minus the flowers. Ava had picked up the three-month-old's dress at an Easter sale and the flowers on Madie Rose's dress was an adorable replacement for a bouquet. But the girl had nothing on her mother. Ava's dress flowed around her, hiding what was left of her little pregnancy. Her auburn hair was up in a loose chignon with wisps of baby's breath.

His girls were gorgeous.

Ava joined him and finally his breath returned. Seeing her had set his nerves at ease and he felt whole again.

"Madie fell asleep ten minutes ago," Ava whispered, blushing.

Jack smiled and kissed her little sleeping head. "She's going to miss her parents' wedding." He chuckled. "Maybe she'll be up for the brunch."

She laughed and nodded towards the priest. "We have to get this done first," she teased.

She hid her face in Ava's shoulder as people stopped by to congratulate them. It seemed like everyone at their brunch reception was more interested in their little baby than them getting married.

"Aw, Madie, don't you want to say hi to your friends?" Ava laughed and rubbed her daughter's back.

"What about daddy?" Jack smiled and walked over with a slice of cake. He set it down on the table, seeing that tiny head turn and look around for him.

She let out a little squeal when she saw her father. Jack picked her up and kissed her little cheek, getting her giggling.

"Such a daddy's girl." Ava laughed and snuck a bite of cake.

Madie's little hands got his nose and tried to push into Jack's mouth. He pretended to eat her fingers. Seeing Jack being such a great father made her fall in love with him even more. Even a room full of their friends and family, they were lost in their own little, happy world.

More to Come...

Kate Sparrows

Kate Sparrows is a Sassy Sue.

She's a cynical hopeless romantic that's in love with her Kindle and book boyfriends. It's really a love that you shouldn't come between. Well, unless you have ice cream, an awesome accent, or an amazing book in your hand. Bonus points having for all three.

Acknowledgements

Forever And Always took approximately three years to write. For that, I know there are many people that won't get the thanks they deserve for helping me and shaping this book. I do apologize if I miss you, and I mean nothing by it.

Big thanks to the lovely lady that put together the book cover. Melody were a blessing to work with and I'm so in love with your work. I can't wait to show off your cover for the sequel!

I want to thank my wonderful family. You've always supported me in whatever I've done. Thank you for calling the Upper Peninsula (UP) home. It's an amazing place that I can be proud to be from.

I want to thank my blog readers. I was just a Silly Sue putting up chapters and hoping they were interesting. You're the ones that showed me that this story was going places. Jack and Ava's story has come a long way since those days and has changed a lot as well. I do hope you enjoyed the completed and final version.

There are some amazing people that I work with while I moonlight at my day job. None of you actually made it into the story, but you each helped shaped characters together. Thank you.

To my friends that had to put up with my crazy mood swings during the writing and the long rants about formatting this beast – you deserved every miserable second of it! In all seriousness, thank you for being there and being able to pull me up from the deeper moments in the story, for not questioning those strange and out-of-the-blue things I asked, and for offering to be my beta readers (even though none of you read too far).

I am sorry Dommy, for making you cry. To be honest, I did tell you on the first page that Ava was dead.

www.ingramcontent.com/pod-product-compliance
Lightning Source LLC
Chambersburg PA
CBHW020559180626
46810CB00007B/2570